To life, for being as eternally complex as fiction

Rebecca Reid was withdrawn from school due to illness at four-teen. Being limited in the things she was able to do, she wrote all the time – poetry, stories, feelings, thoughts. At sixteen, she had her own page in the local weekly newspaper, the *Bangor Spectator*, in which she covered anything and everything: fashion, beauty, film, teen issues and more. At seventeen, she became a model, doing catwalk, photographic work and TV. In 2008, she graduated in English from Queens University, Belfast, and she was awarded an Arts Council writing grant in 2009. Married in 2007, she lives in Northern Ireland with her husband and their three daughters. Her first novel was *The Coop*, the first book in her Thickets Wood Trilogy. *Thickets Wood* is the second book in the trilogy, and *Cherry Tree* will be the third.

Connect with Rebecca online:
Twitter: twitter.com/@thicketswood
Facebook: facebook/rebeccareid.thicketswood

First published in 2014 by
Liberties Press
140 Terenure Road North | Terenure | Dublin 6W
Tel: +353 (1) 405 5701
www.libertiespress.com | info@libertiespress.com

Trade enquiries to Gill & Macmillan Distribution
Hume Avenue | Park West | Dublin 12
T: +353 (1) 500 9534 | F: +353 (1) 500 9595 | E: sales@gillmacmillan.ie

Distributed in the UK by
Turnaround Publisher Services
Unit 3 | Olympia Trading Estate | Coburg Road | London N22 6TZ
T: +44 (0) 20 8829 3000 | E: orders@turnaround-uk.com

Distributed in the United States by
IPM | 22841 Quicksilver Dr | Dulles, VA 20166
T: +1 (703) 661-1586 | F: +1 (703) 661-1547 | E: ipmmail@presswarehouse.com

ISBN: 978-1-909718-27-2
2 4 6 8 10 9 7 5 3 1

A CIP record for this title is available from the British Library.

Cover design by Ricky Woodside
Internal design by Liberties Press

The publishers gratefully acknowledge financial assistance from the Arts Council and
the Arts Council of Northern Ireland.

*All characters in this book are fictitious, and any resemblance to
actual persons, living or dead, is purely coincidental.*

Thickets Wood

Part Two of the Thickets Wood Trilogy

Rebecca Reid

LIB
ERT
IES
NORTH

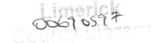

1.

The light is dim. It flickers, not gently, but with urgency. She worries it may be suffocating and pulls her hand back in panic; she hadn't thought that the movement might add to its intensity but it does, only momentarily. There's a wildness in her eyes as she holds her breath, waiting, just hoping she hasn't snuffed it. It settles back to a flicker and she finally exhales but this time she thinks, turning her face to the side before letting out the stream of air; stupidity at this point would be unforgivable. There's life in the shadow it casts on the wall, the way it moves, free life. If only she could remember. The flame calms and she cups it again, more loosely this time. There's a smile on her face. She notices only because the muscles begin to ache, forcing her to wonder how long it's been there. The palm of her hand catches her eye, the dirt all dry and caked; it's not a surprise, just illuminated by the flame. Spit, that usually does it. She works at it for a moment, rolling her tongue in her mouth until a well of saliva rests behind her teeth; some days it takes longer than others but she's lucky, it's one of the good days today. She drips it down onto her hand. It's better than licking it. She wouldn't want to do that. It would only contaminate her mouth and then what would she do? No, she has to spit. There's less than she thinks when it hits her palm but anything will do; she reaches her hand around to the small of her back and rubs it vigorously on the material of her dress, checking it a few times before she's satisfied. It's always the back of her dress, not the front; no, she likes it to appear as clean as possible. After all, that's the only bit she can see, the back is worthless to her. She has never seen her hands in this way before; her lips twitch from their frown.

He gave her the candle because it's snowing outside. It's her only source of heat. He hasn't said it is snowing, she only knows because the wind blew some flakes through the vent. They lay for a moment before melting; she assumes that the cold of the concrete kept them alive. Now they're just drips.

It's short, the candle, just slightly longer than her index finger, and white, except where the ash has stained it. She watches as the drips of melted wax gather over the edge and tumble down, stopping just short of her finger. It won't matter if they hit it; might even feel nice, warm. She huddles closer to the wall and curls her shoulder in as far as it can go, being sure to keep her hair draped behind her; it's not difficult, it's far from soft. She's exactly where he left her, except sunk to the floor rather than standing; she turned her back and sank as soon as he walked away, knowing the pull of the door would blow it out. She saved it, and that pleases her.

Bang!

She jumps, bumping her head on the underframe of the cot. She rubs her forehead where the spring hit her, just above the brow; it's an automatic response, it's not terribly sore.

It was another cell; she can hear the muffled voices of doctors. She sighs – that was before.

★

His legs spun with the peddles, crashing through the puddles as he tore around the corner of the field and down the track. He was going too quickly, his legs barely keeping up with the rotation as the front wheel bounced over the dirt path, twigs snapping beneath their combined weight, sending the water beneath the leg of his trouser. The rain meant nothing; if anything it added to the moment of clarity. He needed it to feel alive. The bicycle shuddered as it aquaplaned across a channel of leaves; the track was thick with them. He gripped the handlebars more tightly than before as he felt his legs flail to the sides, both peddles spinning freely in his attempt to steady himself in the slide. The skid was short, stopping abruptly as the back wheel rode a foot or so up a tree trunk, sending Charlie, elbow and shoulder, hard into the ground. He winced as he rubbed the ache out of his arm, the blood just catching the edge of his vision; he paid little attention, his focus was elsewhere. He dragged it to its wheels and swung himself back on. Glancing, he saw that the tyres were still in working order, for now anyway. He wouldn't bet on them lasting much longer, but they should hold up long enough. That's all he needs, long enough.

Tick-tock. Tick-tock. Tick-tock.

Its face was white. He had never noticed before. He always imagined it was different. How, he didn't know, but not white. The noise used to soothe him, the repetitive rhythm, now it was more of an incessant interruption.

Tick-tock. Tick-tock. Tick-tock.

Before he knew it he was stuffing things into his satchel. What was he doing? He sank to the bed and trailed the jumper out onto his knee. It was purple. He smiled. Reaching in for his journal, he gently thumbed the upper right corners of its pages. They were well-worn, dirty around the edges from battering against all four corners of his life. Worn and bruised. Reminded him of himself. This time he didn't smile.

The clock was driving him mad; its persistent ticking. He'd soon put a stop to that, he thought, lifting it free from the wall and stuffing it into the now empty satchel; already things were quieter. It wasn't good enough. He swung it over his shoulder and charged into his sons' room. Kneeling on the floor, he gently pushed the bag beneath their bed. There, he thought, wiping his hands clean, peace at last.

The boards on the upper floor creaked as he walked on them. They always had but that was annoying him now too, had been for weeks. He'd cast a blind eye, or deaf ear, before, but now it was unignorable. He began down the stairs for a lever to ease them up, that way he couldn't stand on them, the noisy ones, he would just walk on the silent ones, and stack the rest out back for firewood. The wood. He paused. Thickets Wood. His toe broached the outer edge of the third step from the bottom. He hesitated, wavering slightly as he hovered over the edge, the railing saving him. What was he thinking? Sandra would go wild if she came home to hopscotch flooring. He had to get a grip. His journal, that was it. It had become his saving grace. What an appropriate turn of phrase, he thought. He turned to it now more than ever.

'What you get me a notebook for?' he'd asked.

'Thought you could keep it like a little diary, all your recipes and the like,' Sandra said warmly. She knew he'd use it even if he didn't. She was the one stacking the piles of notes together at the end of each week. He'd use it all right.

That was a long time ago. He slammed the bedroom door behind him and knelt on the floor, his weight indenting the bed with the pressure of his elbows as he began writing frantically, every thought leaving him, staining the paper rather than his mind. He wrote for what felt like hours. He didn't know, it was maybe far less, he'd gotten rid of the clock.

He was forty-three. Overweight. Immaculate, or so he would have been had he not let himself slip. Slip, good choice of word. He had let that happen all right, in every department. His clean-cut hair didn't curl around his hairline any longer, it hung miserably above his brows. Two inches longer than ever, and dull. The subtly creased shirts were less subtle and more in your face than was commonly associated with his appearance. Cinders had previously been his excuse for an iron. That, and an effortless replacement for one. They went to waste now, replaced by badly folded creases. She had noticed his slip. She had offered to iron. Presumably he refused, or neglected to care. Either way, he's scruffier than before. He is pale, rosy-cheeked – broken-veined to be exact. A family man, a warm-hearted, hard-working family man with two kids and a wife.

'Charlie, you up there?'

He jumped with the noise, snarling at the interruption.

'Charlie?'

It was Sandra. He remembered now that he was meant to collect the twins.

'Have you got the boys?'

He jumped to his feet, flinging the journal beneath the bed before dashing down the stairs, knocking her shoulder as he passed her on the bottom step.

'I'm just getting them,' he bellowed from beyond the front door, still banging against the frame.

She sighed. It wasn't worth shouting after him, not anymore. His shoes caught her eye, tucked beneath the table in the hall. She glanced back out and caught him before he turned at the gate; he was in his socks, she could see the dirtied soles against the pale tops. Pushing the door closed, her smile faded. It wasn't funny, not really. She hadn't got more than a stifled giggle out of it; there was a day she'd have cried with laughter, but not now, not recently. It wasn't a rushing man's mistake, that would have been hilarious; they'd both have laughed later. No. She knew what would happen, he'd stroll back in oblivious, not a mention of the shoes or the socks stuck to his feet. She'd have to ask to see if he even noticed. That wasn't funny, it was worrying.

It was a fifteen-minute stroll to Mrs Spool's. Walking quickly he could be there in five, or thereabouts. He wondered how late he was. Hadn't noticed the time, that's right, he'd got rid of the clock. It didn't really matter, they wouldn't be set out on the doorstep, they'd be having the time of their lives, but Sandra hated lateness, especially when it came to collecting their children. Too late to think about it now, it was done.

He followed the path along the edge of the wood a little way. He didn't need to, he chose to. It gave him a thrill, made his heart race one beat ahead of itself; he could feel the pounding in his chest, echoing all the way into his ears. Like Russian roulette, he was drawn to it, the risk. He wasn't comfortable, not with any aspect of it. His hands were twitching, his thumb running the length of his fingertips on both hands as he chattered silently to himself, head hung in the hope it made him less conspicuous. He felt pathetic. He *was* pathetic. The fear subsided and his breathing relaxed as he turned up to Mrs Spool's. It took him a moment to catch his breath. He hadn't realised how quickly he had been panting; it left him faint, wavering on the spot while his vision caught up with him. It felt good.

The Spool house was set back off the road just behind Sparkle and Spools. It was quaint and slightly shabby around the edges but she much preferred it that way to freshly painted. Howard had offered his services to them for a day on their anniversary a few years prior, thinking he might be set about painting the place up but no, instead she asked him to do a little weeding and then join her for lunch. Each to their own.

'Hello,' he hesitated, 'sorry, em . . .'

She looked back at him, confused.

'Debbie,' she said with a faint smile.

He knew her name; she'd known him all her life. Her mother was obviously right, she thought, looking at the scruffy spectacle hovering awkwardly on the doorstep.

'I'll just get them,' she said without him asking, stifling a giggle as she dropped her gaze. 'Forget your shoes on the way out, Mr Whitehall?' she asked, trying her best to stay composed.

He looked at her in bemusement, then looked to his feet; he hadn't noticed. How had he not felt it? His forehead furrowed as he puzzled it.

'Whities, time to go!' she bellowed up the stairs, stepping back to let him follow her in.

He chose not to. He was embarrassed as he felt the wet on his feet for the first time; he thought it best to wriggle his toes, give the illusion he was happy with it. It wasn't working. He was mortified.

John's laughter broke his thoughts – a good thing really. He was being too self-indulgent again, a decline he had made recently that everyone bar himself had noticed.

'Tell me you did that on purpose?' he chuckled, Clay joining in, both their fingers wagging toward his feet.

'Yes, yes, boys. Now did you thank Mrs Spool?'

'Thanks again Spoolie,' they called.

John received a quick slap to the back of the head.

'We said thank you properly before we came down,' he grumbled, still rubbing the sting out of his scalp before lifting his hand to the back of his twin's head.

'Ouch!' Clay yelped, more in shock than in pain.

'It's only fair. I shouldn't just get a slap 'cause I'm nearest him!' John grumped as he lead the way down the path.

'Thank you again Mrs Spool,' Charlie called through the door, his feet still on the outer step.

'Not at all,' she shouted above the ruckus of children's voices, her head just visible peering over the top railing, 'tell Sandra I'll be over tomorrow.'

He said nothing as he walked away. He hadn't even heard.

Sandra was right; he didn't say a word as the three of them ambled into the house. He was even quiet as the boys laughed about it, tears streaming down their cheeks as they told her.

'I'm away to see the reverend,' he said quietly.

'What, Charlie?' she asked. He was barely audible above the laughter.

'The reverend – I'm just going to pop over and see him,' he repeated, staring vacantly toward the door.

'It's almost dinner time, could it not —'

She stopped short; he was walking away.

'At least put some shoes on?' she pleaded. 'Boys! That's enough!' She realised her tone when she saw the shock on their faces. 'You're muck up to the elbows as usual, can't be eating your dinner like that.' She smiled warmly in an effort to make up for her outburst.

Charlie was on the front porch already, straddling his bicycle. It was pelting down and he was in little more than a shirt and trousers.

'You'll catch your death.'

He looked at her, really looked at her for the first time in weeks.

'At least pull something more on?'

She'd lost him; just like that he sank back into himself, his weight beginning to bear down on the far pedal as she scavenged for something more to say. It was pointless; she was blank.

'When will you be back?' she shouted anxiously, watching as he eased down the lane of trees.

He said nothing.

The rear tyre was softening; he could feel the plunge of the bike as he peddled to the river.

'It's better this way, me taking charge. Yes, better,' he mumbled with uncertainty.

The rain was easing as he stepped off and manoeuvred the frame onto his shoulder. It was heavier than he remembered. Either that or it just hurt more because of the fall.

'I did it, I know. It's my fault. Stupid, stupid man!' he flustered, shaking his head.

The water was freezing as he stepped into it, balancing as best he could on the larger stones as he made his way across; he had tried to strategise a route as he approached it, a waste of time – you do whatever comes once your feet get in there.

His teeth were chattering with the cold. He hadn't noticed.

'She did it before. Made things right, that's what she did – ouch!'

He went over on his ankle, crashing the bicycle to the ground before stepping out; he couldn't hold it any longer, not with that arm. Its back wheel missed the bank and sank into the water. He struggled with it, stumbling in an attempt to get both himself and the bicycle onto dry land.

'Polly, there was Miss Polly. That was before, a long time ago. Then the Tiding girl, that was recent enough. God, there was her and the boy from the coop, that – that boy didn't come back.'

The air was thick with moths and midges from the moment he broached the water's edge. He waved his arms frantically in an attempt to disperse them but it was useless. Midges were flying into his mouth, he could feel them like grit as he swallowed. The moths batted off his arms and face. Thankfully they were too big to breathe in; the prospect of eating one made midges acceptable. Everything is competitive, he thought. Hauling himself back on the bike he resorted to steering one-handed, his other hand acting as a vent as he wobbled through the trees. She knows, I know she knows, he thought, his eyes darting from side to side, craning his neck to look behind through the clearing to the river as best he could.

He knew the woods were strange now, different. Everyone did. He'd overheard talk of it, chatted about it in the shop, but he'd never seen it for himself. It had been coming, they all saw it. Even those who turned a blind eye knew it was there. He wasn't much of a hunter, never had been, but he heard the men when they came back, complaining of the stagnant air; he knew now what they meant, for as far as the eye could see there was a thick haze of moths. He blinked rapidly to protect his eyes, feeling the thud as they bumped into his lashes. He could feel the tickle as they walked on his scalp, along with the nipping. He was being nipped everywhere. He couldn't see himself but he could imagine he was thick with them, like a moving blanket. He shook his head; they were too close to his ears. He didn't like the wafting and the hum. The air was thinning as his legs began to tire from the pedalling.

He'd been fighting the ache in his arm for too long; it was becoming unbearable. It hurt more as he eased it outward, cracking at the elbow joint in the stretch. The tyres were done, they had been for a while, but he couldn't have stopped in the thick of it. Only now he felt happy to leave it behind, knowing he could breathe freely.

Stepping off the bicycle, he stood straight as a die and motionless. It was then that he noticed it, the calmness in the air; it was limp, just hanging around him, completely dead. It reminded him of his father. There was nothing, not a breeze.

He knew what he was doing, at least he thought he did. Stumbling his way through the trees it became darker, dank. And then he heard it. He knew he would, that's what he was there for, getting there first. It's what he wanted.

Still, it made him jump.

2.

It is bright, too bright. They do something to tone it down as she winces away, shadowing her eyes with her hand; when she looks again it is better, just a glow. It is still brighter than she's used to. It feels warm, not literally, but sunny.

This is her fourth time and her first time to think like that.

She likes it, the place beyond the 'changing wall'. She wonders if one day she might look forward to it.

She's hunched, not through disability but fear. She would stand upright in there but not here, it's too exposing. She keeps her head low to her chest and her chest wrapped tightly in her arms, she'd have had her legs wrapped up there too if she could, but even she knows that's an impossibility.

She spies the corner and scuttles over to it. It is her corner. It's like in there but different. The ground is warm, it radiates up through the floor as she sits on it, her right leg pressed hard against it, projecting the rest of her body into the corner. She makes herself as small as possible, keeps herself tight. It's better that way, she's happier. The wall is pale, soft and dry against the skin of her arm. She untangles an index finger from her clenched hands and touches it; it really is soft.

She keeps her back to them. If she closes her eyes she will forget they're even there, it's not difficult to, they do and say very little anymore. She thinks about what she saw. There's a cot, close to

18

the wall and pushed into the corner; she's pressed beside it now. The table where they sit is opposite it and against the far back wall. There are three chairs but only two of them. She wonders why. There is a rug thrown on the floor. It's pale and furry; she knows more about it than anything, it's all she saw the first three times she came in. She wonders what it would be like to wrap herself up in it. She imagines it might be rough; fur is rough, she thinks, though she can't really remember, not clearly.

She jumps, distracted by the noise; they've put something by her legs. Her face is too tight to the wall to know what. She smells something sweet and glances down, being sure to keep her face tight to the wall. Her peripheral vision is good; she's spent most of her life using it. There's steam rising from a roll. Her stomach rumbles with the scent; she hadn't realised she was hungry until now. She's quick as she snatches it up with her hand and tucks it beneath her still-dropped head.

★

Lilly glanced out the window through the rain, popping the last bite of Howard's homemade bread into her mouth; she missed her summer meadow walks, they were much more pleasant than now. She had already been out early that morning before breakfast, before the rain broke, and it was bitterly cold even then, despite all the extra layers she piled on. She shuddered just thinking about it, pulling her hat down over her ears as she headed toward the hall in search of an umbrella. Howard's trousers caught her eye. He had left them strewn over the arm of the chair for two days now in the hope she would tighten the waistband. He was on a diet.

'It's not a diet,' he'd said. 'I'm not into faddy dieting, I'm cutting back is all.'

It was a diet. Instead of a large bowl of porridge, he had a half-bowl; instead of three cuts of meat he had two. That was a diet whether he was man enough or not to admit it. She had had a great time winding him up, but only because she was proud of him for sticking at it, an inch lost is a year gained as far as she's concerned. It had been her idea; she didn't want to lose him any sooner than she had to.

The umbrella was tucked into the back of the under-stair cupboard. She rolled her eyes as she pulled it free from the array of rubbish surrounding it. Howard was notorious for stuffing things in there. Anything at all that he didn't want to dispose of, but wasn't sure what to do with, went in there.

'The outhouse is the place for these things,' she'd said last year.

'Lou, it's no place for anything that doesn't bend or crank something or need bent or cranked,' he'd said with a grin.

'Oh, I could bend and crank plenty of this stuff!' she'd said with determination.

He knew that voice when he heard it and it usually meant do something about it quick or join her for a bonfire later. She'd done that once, set everything up in a pile and lit it after he left it all sitting around for over a week. She took anything important out, of course, but she didn't tell him that, not immediately anyway. It did the trick.

'Okay, I'll be having them, just set them there —'

'I —'

He knew what was coming.

'I know, I know, don't worry, I'll get them away before nightfall.'

She giggled to herself now; he was a messy old clout sometimes.

Rabbit's Burrow Café sat nestled beneath the crook of trees at the bottom of the village; it was an old-style cottage that had changed very little since the day Mrs Pepperfield's family built it. She converted it into the café when her late father passed away and bought a small house on the edge of the village. The best thing that ever happened to the place, people would say. The interior was as quaint and rustic as the exterior; there was an accumulation of random tables and chairs donated over the years by locals. Everything from lounge chairs to kitchen stools sat nestled around low-rise coffee tables or high-rise kitchen ones. The room was lit with gas lamps and the flames of the fire that took pride of place in a wall all its own.

'Sorry if I'm late,' said Lilly, setting her mug of coffee on the table and dashing back for her caramel square. They were good, but not as good as the ones from Sticky Fingers.

'It's just one of those things, Mertle, always the ones you least expect,' gushed Margaret as she came bustling towards the table.

Her voice carried over the noise of the room; nothing about Margaret was subtle. Her behind squeezed between the arms of the farmhouse chair as she bustled the wrap from around her shoulders. She was always bustling; Lilly often wondered if it had something to do with her size. Lilly positioned herself comfortably in the battered leather lounge chair, slipping her feet beneath her and resting her plate on her thigh. Margaret glanced at her with slight disapproval, giving the pretence it was due to the unladylike position; Lilly knew better. She was jealous. How she'd love to fit her legs by her behind. She smiled back at her, unfazed. There were five of them around the table by now: herself, Miss Margaret, Miss Mertle, Mrs Rose and Miss Petal. It was always a variation of the same people that gathered.

'So back to it dears. Charlie Whitehall,' Margaret sighed,

glancing around them all. She was finally comfortable. It had taken her some time and all the others could do was watch. She was very domineering in her presence; again, Lilly wondered if it came down to size.

'Yes, where is Sandra?' chirped Miss Petal.

'Didn't you hear?' gasped Margaret in astonishment.

Lilly gulped down her mouthful; she was as eager to know the big secret as anybody. 'Hear what?'

'Mr Whitehall—' began Mrs Rose before Margaret rudely interrupted.

'Young Charlie's only away and took off!' she gushed, delighted to be breaking the news.

There was a loud gasp. Lilly just fell silent, the biscuit crumbs slipping from her fingers.

'I'm surprised your Howard hadn't heard,' said Mertle pensively, still mulling over the words.

'He's not one to gossip, likes to let things go until he knows for sure,' she said proudly. It was one of his most respectable traits.

'What are you saying, he's left Sandra?' asked Mrs Rose.

'That's just awful,' sighed Lilly with a shake of her head. 'No wonder she's not here. How's she coping?'

'Ladies, ladies,' Margaret said loudly, 'it only happened a few days ago, nobody knows much worth mentioning yet. It doesn't surprise me, to be honest.'

'What doesn't?' asked Mertle

'That he left her?' added Petal.

'No, not entirely, there was something wrong. Come on,' Margaret said glancing around them, 'he's been out of sorts for months, ever since his father passed.' She sighed, biting into her jam-laden scone. It left a rim around her upper lip; she quickly wiped it clean with the back of her hand.

'You are right there,' said Lilly, 'he was opening the bakery late and half the time he didn't have the same supply. He only did chocolate doughnuts once last month.'

'And the wholemeal rolls,' Petal said, leaning into the table. 'They were the same: over-cooked or under if they were there at all. I just put it down to bereavement. It can do terrible things to people.'

'You said it,' said Margaret. 'There was a vacancy. The man would be standing there, but that fella was as far from the room as the moon and back. Terrible it was, just terrible. Struck me something shocking, Mertle,' she sighed, turning to her, 'but I notice these things, you see, terribly perceptive.'

'Never going to get the final ingredient for that chicken pie recipe now, am I?' Mrs Rose said with a sigh

Margaret was astonished. 'Was he giving you the recipe?'

She nodded. 'Bit by bit for the last six months; I hadn't mentioned it recently, didn't think it was right.'

'Lucky bugger getting any of it at all.' She let it slip a little when she was annoyed. It embarrassed her when she noticed, and she had noticed now, shrugging back into her seat, her face flushed.

'Passed in his sleep, didn't he?' Mertle asked. 'His father, I mean.'

'God bless the old sod,' Margaret said. She hadn't known him.

'That's what they say   '

'No bad thing,' interrupted Margaret, 'the old boy was riddled with cancer, just riddled with it.'

'Did they not try Mrs Pepperfield?' Lilly asked, glancing toward the woman circling the room, a coffee pot in each hand.

Mrs Pepperfield was dumpy. Seventy if a day, dressed all in black with the exception of a long white apron dashed with coffee stains. She was the village herbalist. Some called her otherwise but she was a herbalist nonetheless, had been all her life. Learnt the trade from her mother. A witch, or so they say. Lilly glanced around the walls. Clusters of dried leaves hung in bunches in the centre of each window and high above the door frame; she wouldn't have noticed had a leaf not dropped as she'd walked in. It drew her attention to it. There was a basket by the till full of various bunches with labels hanging from them. Some were leaves, others just looked like twigs. People would come in specifically for them or pick one up as they were leaving.

She had never used any of them herself. 'No good can come from it,' Howard had said. 'You want nature to do its bit; we'll find a way ourselves but no need for that.' She knew what he thought: witch. He hadn't said it; he wouldn't, ever, it wouldn't be like him. But she knew.

He was funny like that, Howard, open-minded in so many ways but there were just certain things he wouldn't hear of and this was one of them. Her face must have betrayed her disappointment; before she knew it he had her swaddled in his arms. 'I've got an old book about here somewhere,' he'd said, the words muffled as he'd kissed her head. He never had found that book, she thought to herself.

There was an old barn door to the back of the till, set off to the right, that people would pass in and out of. Lilly had watched before, wondering. It was her treatment room.

'Far from Christian it is, far from it!' hissed Margaret. 'I'll stick with conventional medicine, thank you.'

She was in the minority.

'She did wonders for John's foot that time.' Mrs Rose smiled favourably. 'Does wonders for most things as far as I can see.'

'Sandra said they brought him but he was too far gone to be helped. There's only so much she can do, she tried her best but it had too much of a grip on him.' Petal grimaced. She hated the thought of illness, especially when fatal.

There was a chime above the door; it created the ambiance of the cafe. Its noise was continual and expected so none of them registered or paid any attention when Tommy Tinkit came in.

'How's your mother?' Pertrid asked glumly. She was in a great mood herself but it was always a difficult situation. Glum seemed the most appropriate replacement to chipper. She was resting on the counter, her weight dispersed between both arms.

'Aw, she's okay,' he sighed.

'Not great?'

He looked up beneath his brows without a word.

'What can I get for you today then?' she continued pleasantly in an attempt to soften the atmosphere.

'I actually came in to ask about Sticky Fingers.'

She looked blankly at him for a moment before it clicked.

'Oh, closed again. He seems to be away. Vanished. Poof,' she giggled, wafting her hands in front of his eyes.

He seemed unimpressed.

'Really?' he asked.

'Really. Dunno where he's gone and got to. We got anything to fill the spot?'

'Any chicken pies?' he asked, his lips curling in a smile as he scanned the goods on offer.

'Nope, but got a brilliant pepper and cheese bake if you want savoury?'

He looked disappointed but agreed anyway.

'I'll take three of the cream buns too Miss Pertrid,' he added, elbow-deep in his pockets.

'She wanted a refill of this if she could as well,' he said, producing an empty brown bottle, 'and these I think,' he added, delving into the basket for a bunch of purple twigs. He sniffed them and smiled. 'That's the stuff.'

'Lavender,' she grinned, placing them in the basket alongside the other purchases.

Lilly glanced to see Pertrid disappear into the back room, her eye drawn to the boy at the counter. He couldn't have been more than eleven or twelve; she recognised him from somewhere.

'There's another sorry case,' Margaret said with a tut.

'Who?' Lilly asked, looking fleetingly at Margaret and following her stare back to the boy.

'Wee Tommy Tinkit. Anywho, did anyone hear any more about the Start youngster having had the flu? Poor wee mite, the doctor was over three times last week and he had her here nearly every day.'

And so it went on.

The rain had ceased by the time Lilly ventured home. Ordinarily she would have cut through the fields but the prospect of being sodden from the waist down was something she'd rather avoid, especially given the cold breeze. She loved winter. People tend to put it third to summer and spring but she loved them all equally. The wind was bitter against her face as she walked down the dirt track, weaving around puddles to avoid soaking her feet. It was a wasted effort, the mizzle in the breeze had her lacquered in wet by the time she opened the back door.

The air was hot, a pleasant surprise. She smiled; Howard must be home. She unwrapped herself where she stood, stripping down to her pants and vest; they were the only things still dry. She bounced out of the heap around her ankles and charged upstairs for a sweater and lounge trousers. The thought was enough to make her burst.

'You're home early,' she cried from the bedroom.

'Wasn't much hope of me getting finished in that rain,' he called. He was in the bathroom; she could hear the water.

'Did the fires light okay? I was worried the —'

'Perfect Lou, don't worry about a thing,' he garbled. He was shaving. She giggled, imagining the face he was pulling.

'Got hot chocolate in the pot,' he added.

Her ears pricked up; she couldn't believe it. Howard's hot chocolate rivalled the brew Mrs Pepperfield put out for the town fetes. He had a trick that she hadn't caught on to yet. He said he wouldn't tell her because then she'd go not appreciating him. That made her laugh too. It burns a little, the chocolate, not because it's hot, but because it tastes hot; that's what makes it so good, a little pain with pleasure. She thinks he grinds down spices but any attempts she's made to mimic it have been disastrous. Anyway, it's his special thing and secretly she likes it that way.

'I'll wait for you,' she shouted, her head now resting against the frame of the bathroom. The steam was rising beneath the door; it smelt nice. It smelt like Howard.

'Get them poured, I'm just finishing up here.'

She could hear the swishing of him drying up the floor. At least he was doing it without persuasion, she thought.

She set the mugs in front of the fire to warm them. She had learnt not to put them too close, having broken a few over the years; she'd made the same mistake while heating dinner plates too. The pot hung from the hook above the fire. She could smell the chocolate steaming through the spout as she dashed about looking for the biscuits she'd baked a few days earlier; you've always got to have a dunker. It was her weakness, dunking. When it came to winter she'd bake batches specifically for it. This time they'd been lemon and poppy-seed. It was an experimental batch and the poppy-seeds were a little sparse but they tasted great all the same. When she found them she set a handful on a plate and rested them by the mugs; the heat would make them chewy. Howard came into the room, a cigarette cocking on the edge of his mouth as he flopped onto his chair and grinned at her. He knew what was coming.

'You ate about five of these today!' she said boldly. She wasn't angry, just amazed. 'What happened to the diet?'

'I don't diet.' He smiled his winning smile, ash precariously balancing as he reached for the tin. 'They're too good Lou,' he added sheepishly.

She rolled her eyes, reaching for the pot and filling both mugs to the brim. 'I know,' she giggled, 'you're still getting a third less for dinner.'

He winked at her. It was a sign of approval.

3.

She remembers it. Not clearly, but in patches. The distinct feelings are gone. Freedom. Space. She let those go. It aches trying to remember. She could feel it, how it pulled at her. She never gets it; it's already gone.

She's nine. Standing in a room six times the size she's ever seen. The walls are pale and insipid. She can't remember the colours, just the tone. A colour doesn't last long, eventually it just merges with everything else, becomes an unrecognisable blur.

She was there waiting for her when she came. She stood tall and slim, stooping forward. At first she thought she was leaning down, only later did she realise it was permanent. Her hair was silver and white, piled high on her head in a bun. It was fastened with clips, lots of small wire clips. There would always be strays. Her skin was pale and tight, with red threads running over her cheeks. They were high, her cheeks, like her mother's, that's what she thought, her very first thought when she saw her. High like her mother's. She wore long skirts and blouses, sometimes with a cardigan or sweater and the same beaded bracelet.

He was different, scared her at first. He just sat in a wheelchair and moaned. She grew to love him, more so than her. He wasn't moaning, he was talking; they understood one another. Six months prior he'd had a stroke. That would be the reason for everything.

She still smiles when she thinks of him. It isn't his fault.

People came and went in the time she was there, not lots but enough. He came.

She's gripping her arms so tightly the nails are cutting through the skin. It hurts but she likes it; it distracts her from what she really feels. That would hurt more.

She noticed him no more than the rest at first. He seemed nice; they all did. She noticed how he looked at her when he spoke, before Granny ushered him into another room. Grandpa would moan.

It was decided before she realised what was happening and had she known, she wouldn't have done anything anyway, she would have believed him. Just like Granny. Had she really known, she would have run away, far away to anywhere, but she didn't, nor would she ever. Nobody did.

Grandpa moaned. Not because he knew – he of all people couldn't have – but because he didn't want the lie to be reality either. He didn't want her in a home.

It isn't his fault.

A tickle distracts her; a drip of blood is running toward her elbow. She watches as it builds up in the crease and wonders when it will spill over. That's enough for now. She lets go. Maybe later, but for now she needs to be somewhere else. Not there.

★

The Whitehall cottage sits within a semicircle of fir trees, each as tall and unruly as the last. It's been a week since Charlie left. A week at dinner time tonight.

'Boys, we're going over to the Spools' for a play day,' Sandra called up the stairs. It takes all she's got not to cry as she says it.

'We're twelve, will you stop calling it that!' shouts Clay.

'All right now, chop-chop, I want to leave in the next five minutes.'

She's exhausted as she parcels the cake she made into a bag and fastens the top to stop the air getting at it. Baking was her vent. Any emotional mishap and their kitchen turned into an industrial bakery. It came from the business, part of their genetic makeup she's always thought, that's why she and Charlie made such a great team. Her monthly cycle always saw a flurry of cakes and muffins in Sticky Fingers. She'd bake the days away and Charlie would load them into his basket and cycle them into town. If it was a particularly bad period of PMT he'd call back over at lunch for a double run. It made for plenty of promotions in the bakery. The locals knew the routine but never the reason. They thought it was sheer goodwill. It used to make her laugh: this month's special.

'Mother!' John's voice broke her daze.

'Yes, I'm with you, let's go.'

'I don't know about this, will you be okay today?' asked Clay.

His brother slapped him on the back of the head. 'That was me who went and said that, not you.'

Usually Sandra would have remarked on such behaviour but it was the last thing on her mind right now. So long as there was no bloodshed, they could do whatever they liked.

'Are you, mum? Going to be okay?' John asked tentatively, wrapping his arm around her waist as they walked down the lane.

'Don't you boys worry about me,' she replied, forcing a smile as she draped her arms over their shoulders. 'I just want you to have a nice day while I pack things up.' She hadn't yet mentioned it and it was far from discreet.

'Pack up!'

'Dad's hardly gone, he might come back any second!' John gasped, pulling away and looking at her in disbelief.

'It's just for a little while. We're going to stay at Granny Jones's. It'll be fun, just wait.' Her attempt to jolly them along was failing badly.

'I can't believe you're doing this. We're not going!' John said, stamping his boot hard on the ground.

'Yeah!' Clay echoed.

'Boys, look,' she said, her hands in fists rubbing the tears from her eyes, 'I can't be around the house and the bakery, or the town, or anything for that matter. At the minute I need to breathe somewhere people aren't all looking at me to see how I'm coping. Please do this, for me.' She knew it was a form of emotional bribery but it was also the truth.

They looked at each other as only twins do and shrugged.

'We'll be happy enough,' sighed Clay.

'Yeah, but so long as you tag a note to the door telling dad where we are. I don't want him to think we've run off and left him.'

'What, like he's done you mean?' she spat. 'I'm sorry, that's not right. We will, we'll do that,' she smiled weakly. She didn't care. She'd do anything.

Mrs Spool smiled at her sympathetically as she opened the door. It was exactly what she hadn't wanted.

'Thank you for this. I baked this cake earlier this morning, thought it would do for a snack.' Sandra smiled, raising the bag and resting it on Mrs Spool's outstretched hands.

'Won't you come in?'

'No, no thank you, I've a lot to be getting on with, you know,' she said, raising her brows to indicate their prior conversation.

'Oh yes, you do. Well away with you and I'll drop them back to you after dinner.'

'No need for that, any time at all is fine.'

'I won't hear of it Sandra, it'll be after dinner and no sooner. Now away with you,' she said, ushering her back as she closed the door.

'Bye boys, have fun,' Sandra chirped in her most pleasant voice. It was quite an achievement; they may actually have believed her.

The house was a mess; it was never particularly tidy but was always clean. It seemed worse than ever as she leant against the door and glanced up the stairs strewn with shoes and discarded clothes. They weren't hers, nor were they Charlie's. She had no intention of packing up the house, not for now anyway. It was bedrooms and bedrooms only. She wanted to bring enough things to do them a month or so, maybe longer. Anything else she could come back for, but her decision being what she assumed it would be, she would be back to pack up the rest of the place soon enough anyway.

The twins' room was as would be expected: a disaster. It meant very little at the moment. There was one rule they always kept – clean laundry hangs in the wardrobe. This made her life very easy. Searching under the bed for a case, her hand brushed something, something she recognised before pulling it out. It was a satchel, Charlie's satchel. She couldn't understand why they'd have it, the boys hoaking through their father's things and him barely gone a week. Her emotions gave way and she collapsed, clutching it to her chest as she pulled it out.

Tick-tock. Tick- tock.

She looked down at it puzzled and drew it close to her ear. Tick-tock. Tick-tock. Tick-tock.

She loosened the buckles and tore back the top. The red of the clock shone out at her. Their bedroom clock. She had noticed it missing the night Charlie left. Clock-watching does that to a person; if there isn't one around, you're quick to notice.

She cradled it and wept. He hadn't been the same, not for months, that's perhaps what made all this so much worse. She had lost him before he'd gone and there was nothing she could do to find him. He died with his father. She saw it happen.

It took her ten minutes to pack up the twins' things; it was a matter of lifting everything and stuffing it hurriedly into the case she found beneath John's bed. Once it was filled she pulled on the zip, but it jammed, forcing her to pull harder still; by now she had both heels dug into the floor, pinching the zip in the forefinger and thumb of both hands as she tugged with every pound of body weight. It snapped. She crashed hard into the wardrobe and sank to the floor crying as the case toppled over, spewing its innards. She flailed her arms by her sides and stamped her feet like a child. It was too much; she wanted to punch something.

'Calm down Sandra,' she whispered, pulling a tincture from her pocket and dripping it onto her tongue. It made her wince.

'That's fine, you can just stay there,' she spat, as she stepped over the mess and crossed the hall into her bedroom. It was calmer. She rethought that notion and decided it was dead, not calm. It had been since he'd left. There was a lingering emptiness in the air, like a stagnant blanket that smothered everything. She hated it. She'd been sleeping on the sofa since the first night he left. It wasn't a choice. There was no option in the matter. Their room was empty now. She looked at the crisply folded linen and decided if he didn't return, she wanted nothing from in here.

Their travel bag was usually stored in the top of Charlie's wardrobe; she checked and it wasn't there. That only left under the bed, which is the most likely place she would shove it had he not been there to lift it up. This time the floorboards were cold as she knelt on them, fumbling her hand beneath the bed, her neck crammed into the frame at an unfortunate angle. It was beginning to ache as her fingers ran over open pages, the edge of one slicing her finger.

'Bloody hell!' she shrieked, stuffing it into her mouth to ease the sting.

Pulling herself back, she peered beneath the bed and saw an open book. It puzzled her momentarily as she pulled it out, then she realised what she was holding. It was Charlie's journal.

She closed it and felt the soft leather beneath her hand, lifting it to her nose and sniffing it. She had never opened it. Come to think of it she hadn't seen it lying about much in recent months but he had been writing in it, she had known that. She flicked roughly through the first half, scanning the pages for anything of interest, any explanation. There was nothing. As she flicked on, the writing became more erratic, messy, it went every which way as though he flung the journal open and wrote without caring in what direction. Then she saw it. Read what he had done. She threw the journal across the ground and shoved herself back against the wall, wiping her hands on her thighs as though they were unclean. It sat for a moment before she crawled back over and began reading again; she had to understand.

He had done the unthinkable and never mentioned it to her. He had never so much as hinted. He had played the hand of God.

She read on, scanning the page and picking up on key words.

The night his father had died, he had helped him along. It doesn't say how, just that he did it.

'I can't even bring myself to write it,' it read.

Then he goes to a place she never knew existed. A dark place.

'She did it before and she'll do it again, the lady, the lady in the woods. I've watched and seen. I know it's my fault. She's there, I know it, she must be.'

Her eyes are cold as she reads on, the tears have dried and been replaced with fear. It all makes so much more sense now.

'I never thought about it until now, not properly. I was as blind as the others, sitting, away from it all, glad it was never me or mine. Now I know better. It's anyone. She came for them. What did they do? No one will know, no one talking anyway. It wasn't right, I thought it was but it wasn't, not really. The Rev, if he knew maybe he'd forgive me but I can't tell him, I can't go telling anyone. Not this. I'm tainted, stained after what I did. She can see it though. She knows. That's what happens when you do bad things; she sees and makes you pay. You get your comeuppance. I want mine, I want mine before she comes and gives it to me. In God I place my trust. He knows, only him and her. He knows why I did it. I talked to him and explained. He let me choose, now I'll let him choose. If I'm to be spared, I will be. If not, it's meant to be. This isn't living, like this, it's a trap and she's snared me. It's part of it and I can see it happening. I don't want to watch, I want it over. Let it be over. Please let it be over.'

If only he'd talked.

The journal sat limp on her lap as a tear warped the ink. She knew now what numbness was.

She raced into the garden, grabbed a handful of sticks, stacking them neatly on top of twisted paper. The ground was damp but she didn't care, she'd make it light whatever it took. There was alcohol in the kitchen, they kept it tucked to the back beneath the sink. She raced back in, pulling everything to the ground as she grabbed it by the neck. It was gin. She unscrewed the lid and glugged a mouthful down, coughing and spluttering; she wiped her mouth and took a second slug. It was potent and hot in her mouth; she could feel the burn all the way down her throat into her chest. The front door was still open, banging against the frame as she crossed the hall and walked back toward her makeshift bonfire. That's what it was, a book bonfire. She opened the journal and propped it over the top before tipping the remaining gin over its back, watching as it soaked into the leather and down onto the sticks. She pulled the matches from her pocket and tried her best to shade them as she lit it; it wasn't working, the breeze was too strong. She decided instead to light something inside and drop it onto the pile. She took the first thing she saw, John's T-shirt, and set it alight. Whoosh! The whole thing went sky-high in flames when she dropped it on top. The warmth was nice. She stepped back and reached out her hands as she watched it burn. She wanted it gone. It was dark, twisted. Her boys need never know the way their father went. She wouldn't have it. They thought little enough of Mrs Christmas Eve, she didn't want to arouse their interest. She meant nothing. It was madness. So she told herself. Part of her doubted; she could feel it, a weakness to succumb to it. It could be overruled. It was madness.

4.

She remembers Granny's face the day he came for her. It was more guilt than sadness. She had told her the night before that she was going to be looked after by younger, more capable people. She was seventy-four with a crippled husband and a diminishing house to bear on her shoulders. She couldn't understand how she made things worse, she was only nine. She hadn't cried, not at that moment. But on the morning he came, when leaving was a reality, then she cried. She wasn't crying for want of her, no, but for him, Grandpa. She was crying for want of him and he for her. It was almost unbearable. She wouldn't realise that that was half the reason Granny was so easily persuaded. Jealousy.

They had to tear her away, unhook her grip from his coat and lift her off his lap. He reached out as best he could but only she knew that; his fingers were outstretched and he cried out with the frustration of being incapacitated. She never saw him again. Thinking of him now, she imagines he's still alive; he couldn't be of course.

The car was musty with dust and dirt. The seat stuck to the back of her thighs. She didn't like it. She stared at the back of his head as he drove.

She struggles with the image. Her eyes squeezed shut. She's shaking her head, not sure if she wants to revisit it. This is the beginning. She hates that she sat there. She hates that she trusted.

His hair was lank. It was unwashed, she knew by the way it hung, and that disgusted her, even then. There were flakes in the roots, pale flakes. That made it all the worse. His shirt collar rode up the bristles at the back, shedding flakes onto the upholstery. She pulled her legs beneath her to avoid them as they drifted to the floor. There was rubbish at her feet, old wrappers, one had an image of a dog on it. She smiled. She would never get one.

'I think that's enough for now.'

The words are no more than muffled sounds. She's trembling so hard her head is vibrating off the wall. Dogs. She feels a little damp; her bladder's gone again. She wants to go back, doesn't want to sit here anymore. Glancing over her shoulder, they're sitting at the table; one of them smiles. She wants her sheet. She'll dart for it. She'll be in there before they stop her.

They wouldn't have tried.

She lurches forward and crashes awkwardly against the frame as she charges into the cell. It hurts but she's here. Her blanket rests on the cot where she left it; it's cold to the touch. She doesn't mind, it smells familiar. She draws it around her shoulders and sinks against the base of the door. Her door, not the one in there, not through the changing wall. She's done thinking of herself. She wants to go away.

★

As soon as they arrived in town people talked. They were different. She looked older than her days; it was assumed, given the ages of her children, that she could only have been around thirty, but she looked closer to forty in the face. There were two offspring, a girl about seven and a boy around ten. Nobody can be terribly accurate; there was never an opportunity to find out. You would hear tell of a baby but it was merely speculation. They were puzzling, her in particular, an insignificant figure in appearance but menacing.

Their skin was pale and anaemic. Greying almost. It added bleakness to their inconsequential existence. People pitied them all the more. Their behaviour was ominous and they were reclusive. Local children peered over the fence the odd time and spied vegetables growing in patches throughout the garden; it kept them self-sufficient, made venturing out even less necessary. She must have picked them after dark, else someone would have seen her out. They never did, just empty patches sparse of fresh pickings. Her children avoided schooling, decidedly her or the husband's influence. They failed to attend from one year to the next.

'Terrible it is, keeping them little'ens shut up like that. Not natural, it's not,' Miss Violet said at the time; she was later to become Mrs Rose.

The husband was too idle to work; much like the rest of the family, he just stayed away. Had he taken a job they might have got a name for them but the people got little more than a shadow cast in the window. She was seen out, or so they thought, once or twice, venturing to the wood, but that was all she gave them. They became nothing more than fleeting images.

Little more than pity was ever uttered toward the children; they were, after all, captive to their own parents. Or lack of parenting, as it were. It ran rife through the village: why they did it, kept them in day after day, month after month. Even the garden went un-played-in. The doorsteps, back and front, were cold from lack of wear. Some speculated they were retarded or inbred, keeping themselves to themselves for want of being discovered.

Others chose a darker resolve.

Christmas Eve, forty-two years ago, the family died in a fire. Not one survivor. They found it on Christmas morning, a cindered patch where the house once stood. People would have felt for them if they'd had cause to, but what can you feel for a shadow, a haunting? She was haunting both in existence and after, Mrs Christmas Eve.

'Like mannequins they were, only not so attractive, clearly,' said Margaret.

She was a teenager when they came. Remembers them quite vividly, or so she'd have you believe. 'Never made any friends, never spoke for that matter,' she said, pondering. 'Seldom left the house.'

'Poor Sandra,' sighed Mrs Spool, 'I had no idea things were so bad.'

'Don't think no one did my dear, not a soul,' Margaret said into her mug. She was on her second refill when Lilly arrived.

'I don't understand. Last week everyone was saying he'd left her?' asked Lilly. She was twenty minutes late. It wasn't her style but Howard had been determined to cook a late breakfast.

'Well he has,' sighed Mrs Drey. She seldom had time to attend the coffee mornings but she'd make it once a month or thereabouts. Any more frequently and she said her husband would put her out of use, and then what would she do with all her time. Idleness wasn't appealing. 'Left her, in a way,' she paused. 'Either way, he's gone.'

Margaret pushed herself forward, her bust resting on the table. It was large like the rest of her. 'Making God's choices for him, would you ever have thought it? Think that was enough to put Sandra's head away, never mind the rest. To think, she thought the old boy just popped it. Imagine finding out he'd done it all along. Pushed the boat over so to say.' There was glee in her voice; she relished the drama.

'Are you sure?' asked Mertle. 'It seems so out of character. He was as nice and airy as they come.'

'That's just it – ones you least expect. Anywho, she found it in his journal so unless he was lying to himself, I'd say you can trust it's as good as gospel. Straight from the horse's mouth, or as near to it.' She paused. 'It's a haven for the darker forces, if you know what I mean,' Margaret whispered, her eyes darting in all directions. People didn't like to talk about it.

'What is?' asked Miss Petal.

'The wood. Thickets Wood!' she hissed, her whisper louder than intended.

Mrs Drey shifted in her chair; she was becoming uncomfortable.

'It's got nothing to do with Mrs Christmas Eve. Nature just changes, that's all,' she said sharply.

'Well the men don't go hunting there no more, you heard what they had to say I'm sure,' Margaret added adamantly. 'I wouldn't go ignoring what nature does.' There was a silence.

Lilly hadn't been to the woods for a while, not since the tragedy. She didn't mind the moths, and the midges she was used to. It was the dead air that put her off. It was stagnant.

Margaret spoke, her eyes elsewhere to check no one could overhear. 'There was always something eerie about them – always. No one could quite put their finger on it, not at the time. They were just dark, solemn, no life about them you see. It wasn't right. People didn't like it. You remember, don't you Mrs Drey?'

She drew her eye from the rim of her mug. She had been running her finger around it, distracting herself. She glanced up in silence.

'Don't you?'

'I suppose. They're not worth thinking about. They weren't right then and they're not right now,' she said. She had been nine when they passed.

'Howard said no one saw a thing, heard nothing either. Bit strange don't you think?' Lilly said. She could feel a chill coming through the crack in the window frame behind her. It made her shudder, creeping along the length of her neck, goosebumps running down her arms. She twisted in her chair and swung her legs closer to the fire. It made no difference; they kept on creeping. It wasn't the breeze, or the cold. She knew what it was, only she didn't want to admit it. She tried desperately to shut herself off from the voice in her head. She knew what it was all right, it was this, right here, she thought, a low ache of uncertainty settling in her gut.

'It's Farmer Cedrick's now, the land. Has been for thirty-odd years I think.' Petal smiled in an attempt to steer the conversation toward the light.

'Folk didn't like the thought of a house on it,' Mrs Drey uttered, 'didn't seem right. He uses it as part of the old farm. Just better that way.' She looked to Margaret. 'The Drey family didn't want it, I'm well glad too.'

There was something in the way the older two spoke to one another: they knew more than they said. Lilly caught it. She hadn't been looking for it but it was there all right.

'Maybe it's no coincidence what happened to those other young'ens?' Margaret said, her voice lower than ever.

Mrs Drey pondered it. She wasn't quick to disagree.

Petal looked surprised. 'Who? That boy?' She hesitated, searching for his name. She found it. 'The Cauldwell boy and poor Miss Tiding?' she said as she sank back into her chair, having lurched forward in interest. 'That's not right,' she tut-tutted, 'couldn't be.'

Mrs Drey looked to Margaret and dropped her glance to the floor. It had passed her mind six months prior, when it had happened. Had crossed others' minds too but little was ever said aloud, not beyond the confines of their own front doors.

'I wouldn't go dismissing it,' added Mrs Spool, gulping down her coffee. 'It was near the wood after all, wasn't it?' she asked, turning to Mrs Drey, a hand placed on hers for ease.

She nodded in response. It wasn't something to be gossiping about, not in detail.

There was no need for explanation; Lilly and the others knew exactly what was being referred to. The point in the river where Jodie drowned. No one wanted to say it, they simply acknowledged understanding with subtle sighs and nods. It was enough. Lilly shifted in her seat, hoping to shake the ache from her gut. The one telling her that they were right, that there was something in the wood, something she had felt time and time again and fought to ignore.

'That's right,' boasted Margaret, 'and he never came back.' She leaned in closer still, her eyes dark. 'Just vanished, like young Charlie there —'

'Top up, ladies?' It was Mrs Pepperfield.

Three of the mugs were raised, including Margaret's. It was her third.

'Be high as a kite after this,' she grinned, raising her mug higher still in thanks.

Mrs Pepperfield smiled and moved on. She wasn't one to stop and chat, not without invitation. Lilly watched her at the next table, pulling a string of seeds from the pouch in her apron and handing them to Mr Stone. He looked hugely appreciative; it was obviously pre-arranged, it was much too quick an exchange to be otherwise. She sat pondering what it could be for. He looked in good health, but then again she treats more than physical ailments, she does more for the mind and soul, or so she'd heard.

'Lilly?'

She was hazy, not listening to the conversation. 'Sorry, what?' she said, turning to Miss Petal.

'Do you go anymore, into the wood?'

She shook her head. 'It's not for any reason other than the feel of the place —'

'See,' Margaret interrupted, 'see, that's what they say. You'd be the first to know, Lilly, off on your wee walks every day.'

'I'm not saying anything other than it feels strange. Never said there's . . .' Lilly quietened her voice. 'Never said there's anything untoward about it.' She said it but part of her, the part deep down inside herself, knew she was lying.

'There's Miss Polly too, can't be forgetting that,' hissed Margaret.

Lilly's eye was drawn to a flickering gas lamp. It made her uncomfortable. She shifted her legs and hugged them close to her chest. She had nothing in her hands. One cup of coffee was enough for her. She was merely there for the conversation and now she was beginning to doubt that she should be.

'I'm not sure that we should talk about it,' she said anxiously.

They looked at her. Miss Mertle turning to Margaret in interest. 'I had clean forgotten about that.'

'She was a wee young thing then, like Bambi she bounced about, always a kind of fear in her eyes. Lovely young girl, still is God love her,' Margaret sighed. 'How long ago would it be?' She pondered, her eyes to the roof as she counted up the years. 'Must be twenty-seven, twenty-eight years I'd say. Imagine, and she hasn't whispered a word to a soul.'

'Doesn't bear thinking about,' spat Mrs Drey. She felt uncomfortable. It was clear by her movements; they were exaggerated, distracting. An attempt to shade herself from the conversation at hand.

She was eight when it happened. Like the other youngsters, the woods were her playground. She'd charge across the makeshift bridge and into the trees, following the paths she knew and ones she didn't. It was fun.

'Want to play let's get lost?' smiled Polly, addressing the doll in hand as she wobbled on her feet, her vision blurry, having just spun in circles. It was a challenge she had with herself: how many turns before falling over. She had just beaten yesterday's record with twelve.

'Bet we can't do it, know our way around too well already,' she grinned, swinging her doll to and fro with her steps. The ground was dry, fresh leaves on the trees and not a cloud in sight. Wild bluebells were scattered around the base of the trunks as she wandered between them, deeper into the wood than ever before. She had to go deep if she wanted to get lost. It wasn't a literal game, she would always know her way out. That was the fun. The adrenaline of panic. She liked it.

Eight hours later Mr Jones and Mr Spence found her in the woods. It was no guessing game where to start the search. They knew, they all knew. They could hear her before they saw her. It echoed through the trees as they crept along, one lantern between them illuminating each step they made and no more. It was creepy, the wood at night, total darkness all around except for the tiny light they carried.

'Don't touch me, keep your hands to yourself, I don't like being touched!' spat Spence.

Mr Jones removed his hand from his back. 'I just don't want you going too far ahead, can't see a bleeding thing.'

'For Christ sake, I just stood in something!'

'How do you know?'

Spence stopped abruptly, rubbing the sole of his boot on the dirt ground. 'Can feel it,' he said, frustrated, still scratching at his sole. 'Bleeding crap!'

'Give me the light and you sort it out,' said Jones, reaching for the pole.

Spence pulled his boot to his nose, his weight resting on a tree trunk. He winced and gagged. 'God, it's dog shit! Filthy mutts, they ought to cover their stools with dirt. That's what they're meant to do, wild dogs anyway, any other sort is j —'

'Sssh!' hissed Jones, his arm waving violently behind him to shut his friend up.

'Listen.'

They stood, still and composed, listening through the creaks of the trees and snapping twigs.

They heard it. A voice. A trace of a voice in the distance.

Spence straightened up; arching his back against the bend he had held. It cracked. Jones jumped.

'Aw shit!' he gasped, relieved to realise what it was.

Spence chuckled but it was no more than that, he was too busy trying to listen.

'Come on,' he said, snatching the pole back and stepping across in front of Jones. His movements were quick, forcing the flame to flicker through the hinged glass. They froze momentarily and held their breath while it settled. There was little chance they could manage to put it out but it would be typical bad luck.

They continued on, fondling their way through the growth for a good ten minutes when there was a sudden thud. Jones fell. He yelled out in shock, not pain. Spence spun around, lighting the area and saw the fallen tree and stump. He had just missed it. He felt a tug on his trousers, he saw now it had been a shard of bark protruding from the base. Jones pushed himself from the ground, twigs and bark imbedded in his hands where they broke his fall. They scattered to the ground as he rubbed them on his legs, a few painful jabs in the motion; he had splinters. It would be useless searching them out now; it would have to be done when they got back. He couldn't help but focus on them as they walked. He didn't mind, it distracted him from the mass of dark surrounding them. They were a wandering glow in a pit of darkness. He didn't want to think about it. Splinters were preferable; he picked at them.

'Sssh, do you hear that? It's close,' Spence said, freezing. 'It's a girl all right. What's she doing, singing?' he added dubiously.

He was right. She was.

They could see the flames through the clearing. It was deceptive; they appeared closer than they were in the darkness. The men rushed forward – they wanted to reach her, check she was all right.

'Miss Shortbridge! Polly!' yelled Jones. 'Miss Polly, it's Mr Jones and Mr Spence.'

There was nothing, just the hum they had heard before.

'Polly!' they cried, charging a path through the trees.

They were reluctant as they neared, slowing their pace to a creep and inching closer as they listened.

She sat kneeling in front of the fire, rocking as she sang:

Precious Polly, precious Polly,
where did you go? Where did you go?
All the way to the woods and back,
all the way to the woods and back.
For everyone to know.
For everyone to know.

She didn't move, her eyes staying focused on the flames. Even when they approached, she just sat still.

'Oh God!' cried Jones as he shaded his eyes. Vomit came up in his mouth; he swallowed it back down and drew his hand away. He had to look.

'Jesus Christ,' Spence uttered slowly beneath his breath, trying to fathom what he saw as he forced himself forward against his will. His will wanted to step back. He wouldn't have it, he was a man, and not just any man, her brother-in-law.

Jones gagged again as he tried to gather himself. 'Come on, let's get her lifted.' Diverting his eyes, he used his peripheral vision as guidance, keeping him from tripping over her as he reached down.

Precious Polly, precious Polly,
where did you go? Where did you go?
All the way to the woods and back,
all the way to the woods and back.
For everyone to know.
For everyone to know.

'That's when she swept through the village, that's when people realised,' Margaret said coldly. 'Wasn't at first. Oh no, years later once strange things started to happen, that's when they realised it. She didn't stop singing it when the doctor came or anything. Days it was, apparently,' she added with a shudder. 'They taunted her about it for years in school. Terrible. Still hear some little'ens rhyming it off today, not to her but in the street, mostly when they've hit the ages that their parents will have just told them. They all get to that stage eventually. Anyway, she keeps them well covered, the scars —'

Mertle interrupted, her face distorted. 'They're frightful, just frightful if you catch a glimpse.'

'Can't imagine what happened to her to end up as she did. It doesn't bear thinking about,' grimaced Mrs Spool.

Lilly sat engulfed by the silence; it was all news to her.

5.

It lingers in the back of her mind. She can feel it, see it, even when she's trying not to. The heat is growing. She loosens her grip on the sheet and drops it to the ground; it's still of use as a cushion against the concrete. The breeze beneath the door is pleasant, cooling in the heat of the room. She fidgets, irritated by her thoughts; there's no escaping them, not now, she knows that much.

It didn't worry her when he stopped the car, even when he ushered her out by the arm and closed the doors. She had no reason to doubt. Nothing had ever happened to prepare her for betrayal. He took her by the hand and smiled – it makes her sick to the stomach thinking about it now.

Her hands feel dirty; she's wiping them on her dress.

His teeth were nice enough; the pointy one on the top overlapped toward the front a little but it seemed endearing. It was the top left, or was it the right? It was the right if you were facing him. There was something stuck in the overlap, yellow, it looked like corn. It made her lick around the outside of her teeth to see it.

She's licking them now.

She hadn't had corn; her teeth would be fine. He took her through the garden. The grass was freshly cut, she could smell it, see the mounds piled on the lawn.

She's trying but the scent is gone, long ago.

The hedges were wild, overgrown and encroaching on the dirt path. It appeared to be there through wear, not intent. Still, he squeezed them along the length of it all the same, her hair catching on the overgrowth as he tugged her along. She felt a yearning in the pit of her stomach by the honeysuckle tree. A curl of her hair caught behind her as she passed it. They were wilting, the ground was thick with them. His impatience shocked her, grabbing the strands in his fist and jerking them free. There was no tenderness or concern in his actions, just haste. He was flustered; she could see it for the first time, dragging her quicker as he glanced behind, again and again he did it, like there was something there only he could see. It crossed her mind to snatch her hand away and run but she'd get in trouble with Granny for being impetuous. What was she thinking being so silly? She wishes she had. It was instinct. She had known all along.

Her eyes are welling up, guilt churning her stomach so hard that her chest hurts. The pangs are intense as she writhes on the floor, gently pummelling her stomach; it makes it bearable. She hates that she created this for herself. That she got so close, too close. Why hadn't she just stayed away from him? She hates what could have been. There are other could-have-beens, not just that, the others, there's them, there's always them.

★

The rain began just as Lilly turned toward the back porch. She ran the final few steps; it was a downpour. Howard's chair had been left propped beside the back door. She slouched onto it, the cold of the wood burning up through her trousers. It was to be expected, the air had turned bitter just before the clouds broke. She had left her chair too close to the edge and already she could see the sheen of wet on the seat; his on the other hand was dry, having been propped in the shelter, presumably where he had a smoke before heading to work. He had left the ash tin beside the leg. She looked out toward the meadow and watched as the shafts of rain pelted the grass, the noise on the timber roof echoed that of the ground. It was pleasant. She clasped her arms around herself in a shudder; the air was too cold to sit there any longer.

Turning to open the door, her gaze caught the rim of trees beyond the meadow. Thickets Wood. She paused for a moment, just looking at it, its shadow cast down on the land. It was dark in the rain but there was a beauty in it, or there had been; now it seemed menacing. More than that, it was haunting. A shiver ran down the length of her spine, spilling into her shoes, pulling down her guard and letting the voice scream in her head. She quickly opened the door and dashed inside, the glass panes shook with the slam but she didn't care, she was too busy fumbling for the key on top of the frame. Her hand scrambled through a layer of dust, fingertips searching desperately for the feel of metal. A heavy breath escaped her as she found it and rammed it into the lock for the first time in all these years.

She glanced at the clock. It was almost four, and she knew by the rain that Howard would be home soon. A smile stole onto her lips and suddenly the notion of the woods felt silly. Howard would laugh. She giggled; he had this strange way of making everything bad go away. He always had. She glimpsed the stove and noticed he had already stacked it, ready to light. Her smile broadened; no doubt he would have done the others. It took the pressure off, she thought, lifting the matches from the shelf and striking one close to the wood. She was dreading the thought of running out in the rain for logs and it wouldn't be just the once, it took three or four goes to light all the fires. It took light and began to smoulder as she headed to the living room. Most days she would do it in the morning but she had been running late. No need to think about it now anyway, he had the hard labour done, which meant she could kick off her boots and settle down to cooking. There were only three matches left; she propped the box on its end and left it sitting on the table as a reminder to Howard. He knew if it was upright he had to get another.

They were having potato and leek soup tonight with crisp bread. It was a nice alternative to stew, only without the meat. Howard was a big fan, as was she. The leeks and potatoes were stored in the cool compartment just off the kitchen. It was bitterly cold at the best of times, hence its purpose, but it didn't help when the kitchen stove was only smouldering. She lifted the pot and made a dash for it. The leeks were hanging directly opposite the door, along with the onions. She swung them over her shoulder and knelt down to fill the pot with the grubby potatoes stacked against the wall. They smelt fresh and earthy as she dropped them in, the soil crumbling in her hands. They had dug them out three days earlier.

'Good harvest of tatties this year, Lou,' Howard had said, grinning from ear to ear. 'Think they'll last the long haul?'

It was his way of joking. She threw an eaten one at his leg; he jumped back to dodge it, ended up stumbling on the potatoes and falling on his behind. She felt bad after that.

'These bones can take a bashing yet,' he said with a laugh as she reached out to ease him up. He took her hand out of politeness. They both knew he didn't need it.

'I'm going to ration myself this year,' she said in her defence.

'Well I'm glad to hear it,' he smiled, flicking a cigarette from his pocket and resting it on his bottom lip as he wiped his forehead with the back of his hand, the packet of matches clenched in his palm.

She had a thing for newly dug 'tatties', as Howard called them. It was her seasonal weakness. The smell of fresh dirt before they were scrubbed and boiled added to the pleasure. Last year she ate so many they were left short. It was a bad move on her part and she was insistent it wouldn't happen again.

The pot was heavy as she hauled it toward the kitchen sink.

'Let me get that,' chirped Howard, tossing his sweater and dashing to her assistance. She hadn't heard him come in.

'How was today?' she queried, resting her hand on his back in thanks. It was wet from the rain and she was glad the fires were lit.

'Great, thanks Lou. Managed to get it half up before the heavens opened.'

He was building a fence for Mr Davis, an elderly man ten years older than Howard. The fence has been in need of repair for a decade but no, he waited until it crumbled before getting it seen to.

'Leek and potato?' he queried.

'Yes,' she smiled, easing the leeks off her shoulder and into the sink; they too needed a good washing.

'Any of your bread going as a sup?'

'Would you ever doubt it?' she said coyly. 'Thought I might add cheese to the mix, see how that turns out.'

'Well if it doesn't taste great at least this place will smell good enough to eat,' he chimed, already in the hallway and heading toward the stairs. 'Just getting a scrub-down.'

She knew the routine. He would never settle for more than a moment or two before washing away the grime of work.

'It's like signing out, makes me realise it's over,' he'd said with a shrug when she'd tried to convince him to put it off.

'Can't be settling myself to anything until I'm fresh.'

She's understood ever since. It's healthy.

The fire was glowing as Lilly set the kitchen table. The matchbox was gone, Howard must have lifted it. They always ate at a set table, be it indoors or out.

'What's a family without eating together?' Howard would say. 'An excuse for one, that's what.'

He held strong opinions about the dinner table that Lilly completely agreed with. Had she not, there would have been problems. He was raised eating around a table; she, well, she was another story altogether, but it seemed right and proper and she liked it. Still does. There's the odd exception to the rule, like birthdays. That was it, come to think of it, her birthday. It was routine now, set in stone since she was young, that they would picnic in front of the fire for her birthday dinner. It was Howard started it, of all people.

She hadn't known her age when she came to be with him. He'd guessed around twelve by looking at her. She had hit puberty but only just, so twelve seemed about right.

'You decide when you want it to be. Take your time now, no rush, you'll be living with it all your days Miss Lilly,' he'd said kindly.

She took her time, a long time. She didn't have a birthday at all the first year they were together, it took her all that time to realise what a season was, see how each day felt. She couldn't just jump in there and plump for a day and a month, she wanted to understand first. She was far from impulsive as a child. Her rationality was both refreshing and saddening. It took a lot for Howard to give her back her youth.

In the end she chose October. She liked how the leaves turned burnt orange and red. That the ground was covered in them. She liked the heat of the fire against the cold of outdoors; it was safe. Picking a day was a harder task; she didn't know where to begin, so Howard surprised her. On the tenth of October he asked her to bake with him; they made a birthday cake. She didn't understand until he popped a candle in it and then she remembered. Her face said it all; she was overjoyed. For dinner he laid a tea party for two on a rug by the fire. There was hot chocolate and apple pie, which are also part and parcel of the yearly routine; Howard's homemade apple pie and chocolate. She smiles thinking about it while she lays the cutlery; it's only six weeks until her birthday. She'll be twenty-four.

The scent of baked bread was thick in the air and by the time you can smell it, it tends to be cooked. She had experimented with cheese and quite a lot of it. No point in doing things in half measures; if it's going to work it has to be strong and if it isn't, well, then it would have been ruined anyway. It's not that she thinks the cheese won't taste nice, that much she knows; it's just that its weight in the dough might stop the bread from rising. That was her main fear. Sure enough, it had risen when she peered into the oven but only a little, enough to give it some body; she's happy enough.

'Something smells good!' Howard called. He'd been out of the bathroom quite some time, she knew by the scent bombarding down the stairs that he was finished. She assumed he'd been resting. He would do that sometimes, lie on the bed and read before dinner time.

'Come on down and taste it,' she called back, the piping hot bread resting on the chopping board as she carried it to the table. The soup had been ready long ago. It sat boiling over the fire, waiting to be eaten. She had been sneaking spoonfuls as she waited for the bread. That was another weakness of hers, pot-spooning. Howard can't stand it, says it takes the edge off an appetite. He would be right.

The stairs creaked with his descent, a fresh smell mixing with the food as he entered the room.

'Would you mind taking this while I fetch the cheese?' she asked, holding out a bowl.

He took it, along with the other resting on the counter; they were hot, scorching his fingers as he dashed to set them on the table. She had sliced extra cheese for the soup to help tie in the bread. It was sitting in a bowl by the sink. She picked it up and jollied over to her chair.

'You do the honours,' she smiled, gesturing to the bread nestled between their plates.

'No arguments here,' he said, enthusiastically sawing into the outer crust.

He hands her the first two slices and takes the next for himself. The strings of hot cheese run in gloops across to the plates. They smile to one another; it had worked beautifully.

'You never told me about Miss Polly,' she said, peering up from her spoon.

'What about her?'

'What happened to her when she was young, in the woods?' she asked, slurping the hot soup in with air to cool the mouthful.

He shifted in his chair, both elbows resting on the table as he peered past her toward the meadow. 'Nothing to tell, Lilly. What's got you talking about that?'

'Margaret mentioned it earlier —'

He cut her off, 'No need to go looking into things no one knows anything about.'

His abruptness was unexpected.

'How can you not be interested? A little girl found in the woods like that and no explanation?' she said inquisitively, her brow still furrowed from his response.

'You have enough dark in your own past without looking into someone else's,' he said, his gaze slow as it shifted from over her shoulder to her face. 'These things happen.' He shrugged, easing his arms back by his sides and continuing with his soup.

'After Charlie Whitehall going missing it started to come about, the stories of the lady in the woods and what's been happening.' She looked at him, pensively. 'I think it's all a bit eerie, the whole thing.'

He knew she was probing. It was subtle, but he knew all right.

'I know the stories, grew up through it, but it doesn't mean I'd go filling your head with them.'

'Last time I mentioned them you told me they were rubbish,' she said, her spoon dropping into her soup.

'I did,' he said adamantly. 'What, five, six years ago?'

'You lied?' she gasped.

'No,' he hesitated. 'I didn't lie, I just wasn't going to pander to vicious gossip. Mrs Christmas Eve is no more in those woods than I'm dead before you now,' he sighed, tearing his bread and dipping it into the soup.

'Charlie thought she was.'

'And where did that get him?'

'Well that's what I don't understand. He's gone isn't he?

'Lost his mind more like. Poor man had a tonne on his shoulders. Lou, it's not always black and white,' he said with a sorry grin.

'I know that,' she sighed, glancing back over her shoulder. 'You still can't explain Miss Polly though, can you?' she added, staring back at him as he mopped up the last in his bowl. 'Or Mathew and Jodie?'

She was pushing it, mentioning them; she knew it.

He looked up at her, a slow, drawn-out trail from his bowl to her gaze. It was intense, weird, as she hovered for his response.

'The poor girl drowned and he left to find his mother. What have they got to do with anything?' he asked softly. He was weary from the conversation but he let her continue all the same. After all, she had been kept from it for this long.

'It was near the wood, wasn't it? Like Polly and Charlie?'

'What has Charlie got to do with the wood?'

He had heard but he wasn't sure she had.

'He went to the wood, that's where he went when he didn't come back.'

'It's nothing but human meddling,' he sighed, the chair legs screeching across the floor as he pushed them back and dawdled around the table to the back door.

'I know you can't explain it or you would have by now,' she said, finishing the last of her soup.

He flicked a cigarette from his pocket and stood with his boot jammed in the door, ajar enough for his arm to hang outside with ease. It was cold, the wind whipping in; Lilly shivered and cleared the bowls as she stepped toward the stove.

'She was very pale and her hair was long, always down,' he said, the smoke filtering out with his words. There was no need for him to say her name, she knew who he meant.

'I saw her out the once, in the wood yonder,' his cigarette gesturing beyond the porch. 'She was cold all right, mute even. She was startled by us, raking past, stick guns a-blazing, tearing through the wood. We thought it was ours in those days. No matter, didn't bother us seeing others in it, but she was a shock.'

He peered back to see Lilly was still there; she hadn't uttered a word. It was unlike her. She sat on her chair by the stove, her knees drawn to her chest to keep warm. That was the hindrance of winter, the cold his smoking brought into the house. Still, it was a necessity and they'd lived with the compromise for long enough to know it was the nearest thing to a happy medium.

'I'd never seen her, not in person, until then. I mean up close. And by the time we stopped to realise who it was we were twenty feet away and she just stood, still as a deer in headlights, watching us right back.' Ash blew in on his shirt, he quickly brushed it off. 'Nothing shut us up like it before. We turned and legged it through the trees. She watched us, I could feel it.'

'What was she doing?'

He shook his head, exhaling before turning to look at her. 'Couldn't tell you. She had a basket. Out collecting sticks or the like. There were definitely sticks but I don't know. It scared me to look at her, so, well I didn't, not really, just what I saw in realising who it was.'

He bent down and stubbed his butt out on the sole of his boot before dropping it into the jar by the outer frame and turning to come back in. The scent of damp air wafted around the room as he closed the door. Lilly smiled; it was a pleasant contrast to the heat of the fire.

'She was different, withdrawn or something,' he said, drawing his chair beside Lilly at the stove, 'and not long after, Stanley drowned in the swell.'

She raised her cheek from her knee abruptly. He had never mentioned this before, not in any kind of detail, simply said his cousin died when he was young.

'It was winter and he slipped into the gorge after dark,' he added, reaching out to place a cool hand on her knee that sent an unexpected shudder through her.

'This is Stanley, your cousin? How old was he?'

'Sixteen,' he sighed. 'It was a long time ago now but that kind of overshadowed us having seen her. Mostly forgot about it.'

'Did it happen long after?'

'A week or thereabouts, maybe more. He was a great lad, all nonsense and antics, I fairly missed him,' he said, pushing himself to his feet. 'Enough of the dark chat. What else did they have to say for themselves today?'

Lilly pulled her hair free and scratched at the roots as she struggled to think of any conversation other than Thickets Wood. She couldn't. She had been an observer most of the morning, knowing nothing more of the village history than pleasantries; Howard had chosen to spare her the dark.

That had been very well, until now.

6.

They sit longer. She's noticed because somehow she feels less alone. Not that she likes them. She doesn't. That, she's sure of.

It could be worse, they could be *him*.

They're female, that's something, properly female, not pretend. She likes that, that pleases her. A smile twitches her lips with the thought. She didn't always hate men. Maybe hate's too strong. No, no it's right, her furrowed brow tells her that. Until then, she was fine, but that was it, that was the end of any trust. That was the end of anything. She knows that now, sitting here. Reflection, that's what they called it, reflection. She remembers her saying it, the one with the smile. That's what this is, thinking.

At the end of the lane was an outbuilding, much like at her grandparents', only smaller. She stood slightly behind him as he fumbled for the keys, pushed into the overgrowth by the angle of his hips; they twisted toward her, jarring her into the spot she was crouching in. It was a necessity to obtain headroom beneath the bush. They hung on the end of a long chain attached to the belt loop of his trousers. She watched as his fingers worked at finding the exact key from amongst the bunch in hand. There was a spider close to where she stood, she took in the detail of its web; it was busy weaving as she watched. It amused her, she had never taken such interest but she was easily distracted. She thinks now it was because of the fear.

She longed for something familiar, something reassuring and inno-cent. That was it. He gripped her arm and yanked her through the door; she hadn't heard it open.

It was mainly dark. A faint light filtered through a side window. It struggled to be seen through the garden utensils that obliterated its way and any chance of seeing out. The tools were similar to those she had seen the gardener use at her grandparents'. She knew little about them; she had never taken an interest.

The smell hit her next.

It was smouldery and thick, the scent of warm, damp wood. It was no more than a shed after all, and it smelt like one.

There on the floor was a blanket, laid out rather neatly with a pillow and what looked like an old coat as a base.

There was a hum. An overhead light distracted her; he had turned it on. He must have, the chain was still chinking against the shovel handle in the way of its swing. The extra light added little to what she had already seen; the walls were lined with shelves, stacked with rusting tins, rolls of old paper, pots, general junk. One section had been recently emptied, traces of dust outlining where things once sat.

'It's not much, I, I know,' he said timidly, glancing around. 'It'll only be for tonight.' Fiddling with his keys, he motioned toward the floor. 'I hope it'll be sufficient. It's all I could get together.'

She followed his stare; at the end of it was the bedding. Her bedding.

He was nervous, unsure. She knew by his need for some sort of reassurance.

She didn't give it to him. She didn't know how.

There's a loud thud. A whooshing circulates through the top of the room. She jumps. Startled. She pulls herself up and backs into the corner of the door frame, her sheet drawn up to her face. She shivers, the surface of her body tingling with goosebumps as she drapes the sheet down over her legs. She's gone from sweating hot to cold. She doesn't understand but it happens, it always happens in the heat now. She begins to grin. It's pleasant, much preferable to the sweltering heat; anything is, even winter. She stretches out on the concrete floor, still warm from the heat, and basks. The pleasure is . . . she doesn't know. It's unimaginable.

★

The Tinkit cottage sits close to the river on the edge of Thickets Wood. It is an idealistic little bungalow with thick stone walls and an acre of field for garden. It was only two rooms when Mr and Mrs Tinkit bought it up, roomy enough, one for them and the baby and the other for cooking and sitting in. Perfect. They knew it wouldn't do to keep it that size, but for the meantime it got them out of the tent they were setting up home in. Over the years they had five children. One sadly passed away but the others grew into a fine collection: Suzie, the eldest, Stan, next in line, Ethan, then Thomas, but they call him Tommy. Rolf Tinkit expanded the place by one room with each birth, leaving them a reasonably sized house by the end of things. It was seven rooms large and all but one of them crammed to the brim with laughter and love. Mrs Tinkit was more than satisfied, that was all she had ever longed for.

Things changed when Tommy was five and his baby sister passed on at just six months old. Cot death, they put it down to, but who can say. These things happen.

'We've got us a perfect family of happy, healthy children, don't you be wishing that away because of one terrible tragedy,' Mr

Tinkit had said, one arm resting along his wife's side where she lay turned away from him in their bed.

'We're blessed to have been so lucky,' he went on to say. She shrugged him off and pulled away, closer to the centre of the bed and further from him. She couldn't stand to hear the words. They weren't blessed; they were ruined. She was ruined. He wouldn't understand, he couldn't, he was a man. Men don't know the tie between a mother and her little'en; they know nothing about the pain. Her heart ached like it had been torn out and all he could tell her was how lucky they were. She didn't want to hear it, so she didn't. Not a word. She ignored him when he spoke, watched as he moved through the house and turned away in hatred. He had done all this; he had put them here. She couldn't stand to look at him let alone fulfil him when he tried. He would letch at her, or so she thought. Throw himself on her and grunt. She lay there limp and withdrawn, turning her face to the pillow when he went to kiss her. It made her feel sick, the thought of his mouth on hers, his tongue in her mouth. The pungent, thick breath made her retch.

He was Satan and she was the Virgin Mary.

Her arms lay dormant by her sides as he eased her night dress up and slid inside; it was less of a slide and more of a dry shove. He had to force it; there was nothing there wanting him in, encouraging. Nature was against him. It made her bite her lip and grip the bed sheets not to yell out and push him away. It was empty and soulless. It hadn't been, before, but she can't remember before. She's tried, tried to imagine how happy they were making the other babies, how in love and as one they had been. She can't grasp it anymore, can't even begin to see how she had felt that way. Things had changed. She had changed. He nuzzled in her neck, unbuttoning her dress and fondling her breasts with his tongue. It made her cringe; she couldn't help but edge away, raising her shoulder to nudge him off. He would grunt and sweat until he was finished then collapse on top of her. She would lie there for a second and no longer, less would be too obvious but more would be unbearable. She shrugged him off, his limpness heavy on her frame as she pulled herself free and went to the toilet. She did that, went to the toilet as soon as he was finished, not because she needed to pee but to wipe herself down. His dry saliva felt caked to her skin, his sweat tarnishing her nightdress. It was revolting. Wrong. He must have known, felt her dead weight beneath him, his body untouched by her hands. Either way, he didn't care, he had his way anyway. It wouldn't be often now, two, maybe three times a month, a far cry to how they were before but he gave up trying to rekindle that and settled for what he got. The other times he sorted himself out. She wished that would satisfy him all the time; there was no luck of that and she knew it, just thanked her God it was as seldom as it was.

Rolf was a good man, but there's only so much a good man can take before the cracks begin to surface. He plastered over them well enough initially, pretended not to see or care, but it didn't last. He couldn't pretend all the time; it was wearing him thin, the pretence of happiness in a marriage as dead as their baby. She spent two months in bed after little Lila's death, a solid two months. He stepped up to the mark; washed and cleaned the kids and house, cooked the meals and still managed to do his manly duties. It was bearable, just, but on the sixth month when things were little better, he turned elsewhere for comfort. She was up and about but that was it, there was nothing but numbness radiating from her, a cold numbness. He'd see her smile at the children then recoil her affection when he looked for a share. She'd tear her hand away if he placed his near, her voice would change from soft to sharp and her nerve would snap like brittle. She wasn't the only one suffering but you wouldn't know it to look at her; the world bore heavy on her shoulders. It was heavier still on his. He could see her for what she had become, see from the outside what she couldn't. She sat in the centre and stared out of the glass bowl she lived in; all she saw were the lackings, his lackings. He stood, smearing the glass peering in. That was how he saw them. That was how they were.

At first he drank to comfort himself in the evening when the children were in bed and it was just the two of them. It made it easier to overlook the lackings. He would drink and she would vanish. This didn't last, it spread to a morning tipple, helped all the more with her rejection between the sheets and her leering before he left the house. She saw it as selfishness. Little did she know. He was far from secretive about it, kept the bottle tucked in his boot, his right boot. The laces would always be hanging loose, that was how the children noticed. It didn't bother them at first; he was jolly, if a little off balance most of the time but it kept the peace and they ignored it. Tommy was too young to remember him any other way.

'You seen my hat Ethan? Had it last night didn't you? You been playing with it again?' he asked with a slur.

'I gave you it not half an hour ago, said you were wanting it for work.'

'Well,' he said, staggering back as he placed his hands on his head, 'does it look like I have it now?'

Ethan shook his head. Their father had become unpredictable. He forgot things and lost his temper. He stepped back toward the door a little to be at a safe distance.

'It's in here, Rolf,' Mrs Tinkit cried out from the bedroom, she was laid up, had been for a week.

He strode toward the door, banging into the frame as he entered and snatched it from her hand. 'Bloody hat!'

'Away you go and be leaving the kids to it. Not their fault you can't remember your own name.'

He tut-tutted as he staggered out, his hand resting on Ethan's head with a loving ruffle as he passed. 'Your old dad's not up to much son, is he?' he sighed.

He always made good in the end.

As the years went by there was little change, he became the person the drink created and anything from before vanished in the bottle. His mind slowed and he slept more than he ought to but the transition was a gradual one so few noticed his decline. His stomach swelled to a stretched mass that irritated him as he moved, and itched ever more than the rest of his skin. He would sit and scratch, one hand up his jumper, the other dangling a bottle.

Mrs Tinkit detested him more than ever with the disgusting mess he had become. He yellowed with the drink, the children joked that the whiskey was dyeing his skin. Something was dying all right, but it was a lot more than his skin. He kept it to himself when the blood started coming up. There was no need to share it. Who would want to know? She would stare right through him like she always did and take the bottle away again. He couldn't have that; and the children, well they'd just worry.

He could do it himself, tear himself away. He was a strong-willed man, had been all his life. If he wanted to do it, he damn well could. It wasn't easy. He hadn't accounted for the shaking; it was unbearable, played havoc with everything. At first it was dropping things in work. Cost him part of his wages, but he could deal with that, bit of extra time here and there would make it up. The tremors meant he couldn't even pee standing up; instead he sat. Like a woman. It was effeminate and emasculating. There was no choice in the matter, it was that or sprinkle his trouser legs with piss; he chose hygiene over manhood. Then his cutlery began landing by the foot of his chair. It was the last straw. He ignored it at first, shrugged it off, but the humiliation became too much; in the end he ate with his fingers.

He was a sitting pig. She watched him itch and scoff. It repulsed her.

Finally he found a way to stop the shaking, ease it at least – a shot. A quick shot helped it subside. Not as bad as constant drinking, so that's what he did: a shot here and there to give himself some peace.

'You're a disgrace, sitting there like some old man. Better off on the bottle than this,' she spat, kicking out at his shuddering foot.

He ignored her. He knew what he was doing. Coming off it.

They found him the following Thursday, crouched on the floor with his head in his hands. He was dead.

'Oh God!' cried Suzie as the vegetables hit the ground and she ran to her father on the floor.

He looked as though he were praying, both hands cradling his head. She could see the wound as she pulled him over onto her lap, his skin more yellow than she had noticed before, his face swollen, perhaps from the impact, perhaps fluid.

'I think he fell,' she burst out to the boys as they filed in, her skirt sodden to her legs as she knelt scrubbing the blood from the wall.

It seeped as she scrubbed; the porous surface held more than she thought.

It took forty minutes.

They struggled for some time to decipher what had happened, following the traces of blood from the kitchen counter toward the small walkway into the living area. He hadn't made it that far. The blood-soaked wall broke his second fall, or so they assumed. It was only logical. He had been searching out the gin; it was their mother's choice of drink, not his. His empty bottle sat on the worktop close to the first spot of blood. He had reached it though, the bottle; it lay strewn by his leg, blood smeared on the glass.

Their mother was in bed. She had been the whole time. Unmoved.

She ignored the banging of his falls, the wails of the children as they found him. She was numb to it. She couldn't care, not really. She would pretend to, a little at least, any more would be too hard to inject with any genuine emotion. She didn't have the energy. He was her source of misery and now he was gone. She grinned a little as she tugged the duvet above her head to drown out the noise. She was silently pleased. It was a private moment of joy. Hers and hers alone. Maybe now she would improve, see more light in her dismal days. She wondered if him leaving was all she ever needed. She would soon discover it wasn't, but for now it gave her comfort.

'Mother please,' cried Suzie tugging at the bed sheets. 'Please come and see him.'

She kept her back to her and shrugged away. She wouldn't see him. She didn't have to.

The children found the reverend and did what they could to organise their father's burial; their mother was incapable.

He had been a good man, Rolf Tinkit. Misunderstood in the latter years by a wife who despised him for her pain and overlooked his. He appeared strong because he had to – for her, not for him – and she saw it as heartless. He never realised that. Seven years, seven years to go from happiness to this.

7.

The air is thick with it. The smell. Before she can even see it she knows what's coming. Her back is to them when she hears the clink. They've set it down. Closer than usual. She doesn't like that; she pushes her thighs hard into the ground, her arm squeezed tighter between herself and the wall.

The faint dragging sound woke her. It was dawn. She knew because she could see more than outlines. Not like before. Not like in the night. The movement frightened her. It wasn't fast like she knew a mouse could be but slow and heavy. She knew what it was. The tail gave it away. She jumped, banging into the shelving beside her. She froze, holding her position, motionless. Nothing fell; she heaved a sigh of relief. She had been meticulous in her positioning for sleep. What a waste that had been. She had spent her time sweeping around the floor with the broken brush head she found propped against the door frame. There were cobwebs in the roof, plenty of them, all the spiders dead bar one who didn't bother her in the slightest; it was the thought of the other tiny spider corpses that made her squirm. These she left where they were, making sure to position the bedding well clear of them, in case they should somehow fall on her while she slept. The tucking-in had been the next challenge.

She grabs the sheet beneath her thigh and drapes it over her legs, tucking it tightly between her knees. The scent wafts in the movement. Her stomach lets out a groan.

There could be no gaps, not one. Not for any four-legged creature (or more as the case may be) to crawl through. She worked her way from the feet up, tucking the blanket in close and tight beneath her limbs until she came to her neck. She would have had her head in but the blanket came short.

The rat disappeared behind a gardening jacket, hung close to the shelving near the entrance to the shed. She imagined there was a hole there that it crawled through, it must be that. No. She shook her head in absolute disbelief, not a nest. A nest would be an improbability. She knew even then how to lie to herself.

It was the fumbling of keys that woke her next. A sharp pain stabbed in her neck as she struggled to raise her head. She had fallen asleep on watch, her head had hung limp and the muscles now struggled to lift its weight. She heard the lock slide through its bolt hole before he appeared. He was little different to yesterday, the bowl of porridge shaking in his grip as he handed it over.

'I've never done this before you know.'

She remembers him saying that because she remembers the pity she felt for him. Still does. He wasn't to know.

There was no honey, just porridge. But how was he to know how she liked it? Still, it tasted good after such a long night.

'I thought it better than a home.' He pulled a vial of sugar from his trouser pocket and set it on the ground beside her foot. 'Awful what you hear happens in those places.'

She heard the bolt again as he left.

It tasted all the better. Sugar worked almost as well.

The spoon is cold to the touch. She drops it back. It is nothing but a hindrance anyway. She wonders, glancing at them though her peripheral vision, how they knew. Why porridge?

Enough of that. Enough of before, she thinks, her fingers slipping into the hot slop.

★

The news of Rolf Tinkit's death spread through the village like wildfire. They had seen it coming, a few of them, but to the rest it was a shock.

'A grafter, that's how I would describe the man, an all-out grafter.' Howard shrugged, ploughing the stick into the grooves of his boot. 'Too many mouths to feed not to be. Worked as a labourer in the fields yonder, anyone's field.' The mud sprang loose and flicked toward the undergrowth of the hedge. 'Don't think it was a chosen occupation, think he had to when Mrs Tinkit, well she wasn't that at the time of course, but when she fell pregnant with young Suzie. Think it was all he was good to do,' he added with a heave, forcing his foot toward the sole of the boot. 'A bit rough around the edges but a tough life does that to folk.'

He smiled at Lilly's inquisitiveness. She was an understander, not an agreer. He knew plenty of those, agreers. They fascinated him. More than that, they disturbed him. How someone can be told something, anything, and just accept it. How they can listen and not think or consider. She considered. He loved that about her from the moment they came together. She always thought for herself. A pain in the ass at times. More so when she was younger, especially at the beginning. At the beginning it was a challenge, even for him, but now, well, now it was a desirable trait in a well-groomed lady. That's exactly what she was, he thought, looking up at her from where he sat on the roadside. Her hair was hanging loose as it usually would were she not working at something with her hands. The dress she wore was pale blue and gathered just beneath her bust. Her jawline was slightly chiselled from this perspective and her cheekbones sharper than usual. She was a woman all right. Not the little girl he remembers back to. She was the understander he had nurtured all those years. He was the teacher, one of many. He gave the laces a final tug before deciding they were tight, and pushed himself to his feet.

She had seen Mr Tinkit in passing on many occasions but never spoken to the man, not really, no more than a polite hello. It seemed strange to her now, knowing he was dead.

'Something's not right about us living so near and not knowing him,' she added, still puzzled by the concept.

'There are lots of people around this village we aren't that close to Lilly. Don't go worrying yourself about it. He had his circle as you have yours.'

She sighed. He was right.

'Things happen in life that no one expects. It changes folk. It's not for you or me to do something about it, not always.' He nudged her with a grin. She smiled; he had done more than his bit.

The funeral had been a quiet one. Not much to show for a man's life, she thought as they ambled their way home. Even Mrs Tinkit hadn't been present; perhaps it was too much for her, perhaps it was just too soon.

'We never know how we'll react to these things until they happen to us,' Howard whispered, his breath warm against Lilly's ear, she having drawn his attention to it with a subtle nudge and nod toward the family. 'Can't go judging.'

Its sadness weighed on her throughout the day, seeing the children standing all forlorn, hearing the stories of the man he once was and the sadness he overcame and dealt with in his life. She glanced at Howard. He was walking slightly ahead of her now, a newly lit cigarette dangling from his mouth as he hummed the tune of a hymn she recognised from the ceremony; she never wanted to hear those stories about him, never wanted to stand by his graveside and say goodbye.

There was a creak in the hinges as Tommy yanked on the door. It startled him. Not because he was frightened but because of the silence engulfing him. He wasn't used to it, quiet. Not with three brothers and sisters. They were away now; Suzie had taken them up to Farmer Drey to collect any earnings still owing to them from before their father's passing. She had wanted Tommy to tag along too, of course, being the youngest, but he had other things in mind.

'You're the youngest of us lot, be good him seeing you, better than just these two,' Suzie said, grappling for Ethan's hand.

'I've told you, I'm staying with Ma. She can't be left alone again today, not so close to us having buried him.'

'She's not going to notice if yer away an hour or so. You're coming Thomas Tinkit, whether you like it or not!' she demanded, stamping her foot hard on the ground.

'Suzie, let him stay with Ma, she's less likely to worry,' Stan said, stealing a sly smile in Tommy's direction.

Stan was the second eldest; that made him fifteen and the only one old enough to be the man of this family now. He knew Suzie was in charge but he was still the eldest boy and that gave him some say in matters. After a short brawl for authority, Tommy stayed.

Suzie had thought it would be easier with three younger ones towing behind, reminding Farmer Drey of the handful she had now that her father was gone. Two would have to do. She had little choice if she wanted to keep Stan's hormonal rages at bay. She would make this sacrifice for the sake of everyone's grieving; it couldn't be on her shoulders to have stirred things up amongst their pack. Pa called them that, his pack. Stan could win this once.

Drey was a good payer, he would have paid anyway, but she wasn't to know that, this was all new to her. She wasn't to know that there were no earnings either, that Mr Tinkit had drunk them all and more. He paid her anyway, Drey. He knew it wouldn't be easy, not without their father. A drunk or not, he was a hardworking man and his family deserved a good start without him.

That was a lie, Tommy thought. It wasn't his mother he stayed for, it was this. He rested his foot against the door and dropped the rock against it. He had pulled it from the line that marked the potato patch, nothing else for it if he wanted to see anything. It was a small outhouse, too small to be worthy of a window, or so their father had thought, so it was a candle by night and natural light by day if anything was to be seen. It had been easier before, before the hinges gave way and the door wouldn't stand open. Mr Tinkit, had never gotten round to fixing it. Always put it on tomorrow's list. 'I'll do it tomorrow son,' he'd say. They gave up asking him a year or so ago, got used to using the potato rocks. The soil stuck to the sweat on his palms. He rubbed them together to free it before touching anything, he wouldn't like to make anything dirty; these were his father's things after all. He wasn't sure how he felt about them being out here, but he shrugged it off. If it helped his mother he could live with it, unlike some other things, he thought.

He had been dead nearly three days before she left her bed to acknowledge he was gone. Three whole days it took her to deal with her loss, or so the children thought. Then the weight of the memories was too much and she packed everything that was his out here. She let them believe it was that way. It wasn't of course. It was the opposite. She lay in bed for three days because the thought of pretending to care was too much for her to bear. Then the urge to rid him from her life became too strong. They had been delighted to see her move, come back to them in some way. They didn't do as she expected and badger her for affection; they kept their distance and left her to her own devices. It was all in the hope she might go to the funeral. She had no intention of going to that man's funeral. Why would she? To hug her children and tell them through gritted teeth how their beloved father would be missed. No. She wouldn't do it. And neither she did.

She paced around the house gathering things, everything from his clothes to the cushion on his chair, and dropped them out here. That's what she did, dropped them, in armfuls. They banged on the board floor, crumpled and strewn, dust jumping up from the old beams and settling freshly on the new occupants. She couldn't care less for them, she'd get round to putting them further from home when she felt up to it. For now, having them out of her sight was a good start. He had been the ruin of her. Good riddance.

Tommy stared ahead at the molehill on the floor. In reality it was larger than that, but for a man's life it seemed little bigger. He hadn't been a material man, his father. Whether that was because of circumstance or something more fundamental he would never know, but looking at all he had left, he could only assume it was in him to be that way. Minimal.

The sunlight caught a glimpse of metal beneath some clothes, the glint caught Tommy's eye. He reached down and fingered it out from beneath some trousers. The leather was tight, encircled with wood on both sides around the butt before leading up to the trigger. The smell wafted around him as he pulled the gun free, still half wrapped in its cleaning cloth, and set it on his lap.

'Hold it loosely like this,' Rolf said, cocking it back as he inserted the rod gently down the first barrel, 'then twist as you pull it back and forth. You want any particles out of there, want it clean as a die,' he said, placing it in Tommy's hand, still supporting the weight of the barrel in his own. The thin shaft of the rod stuck out toward him; he was nervous at first, to touch it.

'Go on,' his father said, nodding encouragingly for him to take over. 'It's easy Tom boy, won't bite.'

He liked to polish the steel, that was his favourite bit; it seemed less dangerous than anything that involved being inside the barrel. It was beautifully engraved; the swirl of the pattern running beneath his fingers. He could smell the cleaning fluid now; gun oil, it was smoky and pungent, forcing him to raise the gun and cloth to his nose for a deeper breath. The muskiness was reminiscent of the times they had cleaned it after a rabbit run. He had only been allowed to go in the last few years or so. He was too young to have patience for it all before that, too young to sit still. Scared them off the first few times he went, but he was a fast learner and he knew the rewards of a good hunt. They hadn't gone much in the last year, maybe once or twice; the shakes were much worse, too violent for Rolf to hold strong through. He had seen him do that in the past, tense up to keep the gun steady. Thought it was just nerves, being so young and naive, but Stan put him straight quickly enough. 'Ain't nerves making him quiver like that. It's being a drunk.' They had been disappointing hunts.

'Damn this bleeding gun!' Rolf yelled, butt in one hand, barrel in the other, forcibly attempting to bend it over his thigh. He didn't like mis-aiming. He liked it even less in front of his boys.

'Always gotta keep a clean weapon. My pa taught me all this and you'll teach yours one day,' he'd smiled. Tommy smiled down at it now and draped the cloth gently back over it. Maybe one day when Stan's a bit bigger they'll go on a rabbit run again.

He rummaged further into the pile of clothes and came across his father's work boots. They were big, clumpy, industrial-looking things beside everything else in there. He dragged them toward himself, their weight pulling him forward onto his knees. They looked big enough for a giant. He pushed himself up and slipped a bare foot inside, being sure to rub it down to free any stones and grains first. They were as big as they looked. Giant. He recalled the times his father would come staggering in from work. He didn't always stagger of course, but for Tommy he did. He couldn't remember back before the drinking started. He'd stagger in, all mucky boots and baggy trousers, two piglets under one arm and a box beneath the other.

'Got some room in the plate warmer for these here wee'ns Gracey?'

That is his mother's name.

'Rolf, how many times – be taking those boots off before you come entering this kitchen! I don't clean it out for no reason, just so you can come banging dirt in with every step.'

He'd trot on past her still full of the excitement and open up the door to the bottom of the oven. It was a small door to the bottom right, it was kept mildly warm, good enough for plates but not too hot for keeping any young the farmer needed help with warm and well. He'd slip them in gently, leaving the door half-open for them to wander out when they weren't sleeping. They slept most of the time from what Tommy could remember and once they were up a bit and past that, he'd bring them back to the farm.

He wobbled. The weight of the boot on the bottom of his small leg was too great. He tried to lift his foot, boot and all, and this time he fell, crashing into the wall. It was no use, he couldn't walk in them. He slipped the boot off and dragged them over to the side, to stop them obstructing his view. He rummaged on, then he heard it. The chink. He knew what it was before he saw it: a bottle, two. He wished he hadn't seen them; it reminded him. The guilt was still there.

'Tommy, you out here?'

He jumped; again the silence had been the culprit. So easy to adjust to.

'Tommy?'

The voice was getting closer. She was inquisitive rather than angry, judging by the tone.

'Tommy what are you doing out here?'

She had an idea what he was doing but she wanted him to tell her. She stood smiling down at him, her gown held closed by her tight grasp around her waist. It was small enough, she had little appetite. He looked up at her, his blue eyes bright against the dark of his lashes and hair. He was tall for the age of twelve, as tall as his elder brother Ethan. He would take after his father in that department, she could tell by the cut of his trousers just above the bone of his ankle as he raised himself to stand before her. He had outgrown yet another pair; it seemed only a few weeks ago Suzie came asking where she could get him ones that would fit. She kept all the outgrown clothes in boxes in the outhouse. It seemed the only place with room for them. Tommy was unfortunate enough to be the youngest boy of three, meaning all his clothes were on their third wear. Still, they were new to him. Suzie's clothes still sat in boxes with the rest. They never got the opportunity to have their second wear although they should have. She knew now they never would, knew years ago they wouldn't, not if she had her way, but she didn't have it in her to get rid of them. It wouldn't seem right. Would be like throwing away the ghost of what could have been.

Tommy stood open-mouthed. She had let go of her gown, lost in thought. She was clothed, but barely. He gathered it for her and held it clenched in his hand, arm drawn out from where he stood.

'Sorry son,' she said with a sigh, it didn't bother her, or surprise her. 'What was it you were doing?'

'Looking through Pa's things.'

She knew it.

'Just don't be bringing any of them into the house with you. That's all I ask,' she said, ruffling her fingers through his hair. He was a good boy. He had to grieve and she knew she had to let him. All of them.

8.

The screeching of a chair makes her jump. She had heard it before, the noise it makes when they push it back along the floor. She licks the last drip of porridge from her finger and wonders if the sound is as loud to them as it is to her. They never seem to notice.

It was a long day spent wiling away the hours in the containment of the shed. Long and quiet. There were no voices, just the odd car passing in the distance. Cars don't rattle but his did. It came and went a few times in the day but that was it. She sat there wondering, wondering what he had meant by 'I've never done this before.' Never taken someone? Never brought them here? It made her nervous.

She's hitting her head where it rests against the wall. Not hard but enough. Silly girl. Silly girl. She doesn't like it here anymore, wants to be away. Back, in there. She used to always be in there. The cot. She grips the sheet in her fist and darts for the door, falling to her knees just before the frame and rolling beneath it. She gasps for air – she's been holding her breath.

It was dark before she saw him again and even then she didn't really see him. This time he didn't turn on the light, just closed the door and stood in the dark. She wasn't even sure it was him at first. 'I'm sorry,' he said. The voice was the same; it was him. He lunged forward and pulled something over her head, cinching it in tight at the bottom.

She's scratching at her throat, pulling at the skin. She can feel it, the tightness. Needs to check it's not there, needs to feel it's free.

Her hands were pulled behind her back and fastened before he lifted her into his arms. She cried out but the more she cried the harder it was to breathe. It was hot. Suffocating. The material went into her mouth and stuck to her tongue. She had no hands to pull it free. She coughed and spluttered to get it out, then did the same thing all over again. This lasted three attempts. By then she was dizzy and weak.

Her hands are clenched around her throat, gripping. Tighter. Tighter still. She can remember, remember exactly how that felt. She's squeezing. Hard. She begins to cough, not noticing the hand gently easing her own free of her throat. She's gasping for breath and there isn't enough air. A smile is turning up the edge of her lips; that's exactly how it felt.

There was a hard thud as he dropped her down, she didn't know where at first, until she heard the slam. She was in the car. There was a smell, a distinct smell of oil, a petrol canister or something – she was in the boot. The start of the engine was muffled, smothered by the bag and the boot but she knew they were moving. The tyres purred against the tarmac. A soft, constant purr. It was soothing. That, the smell, the lack of air. He was talking, she could hear his voice but not the words.

★

Every day was the same, leaves everywhere. Lilly didn't mind in the slightest that they covered the porch or the front step but Howard, he had his limitations.

'There isn't a thing wrong with nice crispy leaves but when they're carpeting the inside of the kitchen, something has to be done about them,' he'd say. That would be it; he'd be out with the shovel and a sack clearing them into a compost pile.

She swept the leaves off the top of the chair before setting it out by the table, it had a layer on it like a blanket, she used the length of her arm to clear it before settling herself down to watch the leaves batter against the fencing of their garden, fighting their way to the freedom of the fields. She followed their path across the blustery meadow when something caught her eye, not just the shadows of the trees, but a movement, she was sure of it. Her stomach jumped. It was small and fast but an uncertainty rippled through her in its aftermath. She was seeing things. She was. She must be. There was no woman in the woods; that was ludicrous. She glanced over her shoulder to see Howard. Just the knowledge he was there would be enough to settle her, but the kitchen was empty. Her eyes darted back to the woods as she eased herself off the chair.

A breeze swept directly across where she stood, frozen. It was colder than usual but Howard had just said yesterday he thought the weather was on the turn. 'Got that feeling in the air today Lou, winter's here all right,' he smiled, appearing in the doorway. She turned slowly to see his face, it was aglow with happiness. She needed it to seep inside her, into where this dark thing was nestling, and wash it all out. She longed for it to. For him to just take it all away. But once you've heard something, you've let it in.

No one can undo that. Not even Howard, she thought.

He adored winter, as did she, but sitting wrapped in her sweater and pants, it wasn't ideal. Despite the cold, she wasn't going in just yet. She needed to stay out here. She sank onto the chair, drew her knees to her chest and pulled the jumper down over them. It acted like a draft excluder, except for the odd waft that blew up between the slats of the seat. She tucked it beneath her as best she could but even this tent wasn't big enough for that.

'You wanting to eat outside today?' Howard called through the back door, slight scepticism in his voice.

She laughed. She may love all seasons but that was too much even for her. 'No,' she replied, her eyes still fast on the trees, 'I'm just coming.' The leaves crunched beneath her feet as she padded her way toward the kitchen. She never wore shoes, even in winter. It was awakening to feel the crispness against her skin, the crackling was more than just a sound this way, it was a feeling she loved.

'Be wiping those feet before you come in now,' he called, knowing full well she would track in leaves stuck to her soles and tell him it was part of nature. She smiled toward the closed door, her hand pulled free of the sleeve as she swept the pieces from her feet, then cleared the barrier from before the door while she was at it or her effort would have been superfluous.

'Honey oat pancakes?' he grinned, the spoon dripping on the counter as he dolloped the mixture into the pan.

She looked at him suspiciously. 'Thought those were a winter breakfast?'

'Told you yesterday, it's on the way.'

She smiled.

'No harm in testing them out a bit early,' he added. 'Good to prepare the stomach for what's ahead.'

She glanced at the table. There was nothing to do; Howard had corrected her setting while she was outside.

'Settle yourself.' He knew her too well. She was always keen to help, keen to be involved, but there was nothing for it. She sank onto the chair and waited.

'Are you still clearing the Pattersons' yard today?'

'Most of the morning, then on to fixing up the wall. Terrible what a fallen tree can do. Be a great stash of wood though. Keep us going a few months I'd say.'

He flipped the last pancake onto the plate, trickled them in honey and set them on the table.

'These'll keep you going until lunch, that's for sure. Oats, flour, milk and honey. Nothing like it. Even added a wee pinch of cinnamon,' he grinned, slipping the cloth from his waist and sinking into his seat.

'What about you?' he queried, a mouthful of pancake slipping in as the 'you' came out.

'Thought I might get around to mending those few things,' she tilted her head toward the small pile resting on the edge of the settee. 'Have to get a few bits from Sparkle and Spools first but the —'

A loud whistle tore into the room.

'Oh,' said Howard, 'almost forgot.'

Jumping up from the table he lifted the kettle off the hob, steam shooting from the funnel, water spewing from the lid. Lilly laughed. It was quite a sight to see him hopping around, scorching hot kettle in one hand, water spluttering everywhere. It was quick to settle as Lilly rose to lift the waiting mugs onto the table.

'Get a mouthful of that and tell me what you think,' he beamed, clearly proud of himself.

It was scorching but she slurped in a healthy enough mouthful to get a good taste for it. 'Mmm,' she murmured mid-swallow. 'That's new, what is it?'

Howard lifted the lid and pulled at a fine string hanging loose to the outside to reveal a muslin pouch knotted at the neck. 'Thought I'd take some of the herbs we strung up and try them as a tea.' He lifted his mug and took a sip. 'Needs a bit of work but that's quite nice.'

'I like it,' Lilly added, having another quick sip before setting it down in favour of the pancakes; a liquid breakfast would not suffice.

'Got some mint, well mainly mint to be honest because it was likely to be the nicest, with a few leaves of lemon thyme. Refreshing, I thought.' He smiled. He was pleased.

'I'll be back and forth this morning dragging up the chunks of tree but once it's all here I'll be down there until dinner time.'

'Never know,' Lilly grinned, 'might even get some nicely mended clothes to wear tomorrow.'

He smiled back, her face flickering, reminiscent of the younger one he knew before. He remembered teaching her how to sew. Most girls learn young but she was different, she was an exception. It had been a job at first getting her to hold the needle, but she trusted him well enough by then to settle close and learn from him; they had been together two years at that point, maybe longer. There had been bigger things to deal with over that time; it was one of the small afterthoughts that came about by itself. She loved it, sewing. The independence it gave her being able to mend her own things.

That sheet of hers was the first thing she worked on. It was like an operation, she went about it so tentatively and seriously. It didn't look much better in the end, to be honest, but at least it wasn't torn and holey, more of a crumply, gathered rag. She loved it all the same. The final step was getting rid of it; she never looked back after that.

'Yep Lou,' he smiled, placing the knife and fork together on his plate, 'be like getting new ones.'

Sparkle and Spools was right in the centre of Thatchbury, it was a good stroll on foot but much quicker by bicycle; she decided to take the bicycle. There was a steady breeze as she followed the path toward the village. She considered veering right and cutting through the fire roads in the wood, staying sheltered beneath the trees, and then she hesitated, wobbling slightly as she slowed. That little voice was nagging in the back of her mind, telling her to stay away, that there was something not right in there. No, she thought, cutting right, down the lane running parallel to one of Farmer Cedrick's fields, it's nonsense. The air was cold and crisp as she neared the turn that broached the first throng of trees, no sign of dampness to encourage the midges so fond of lingering on the edge of Thickets Wood. Pushing down faster on the pedals and holding her breath, she crashed over the rooted ground into the gritted air. She had been wrong. So wrong. Her eyes blinking hard to clear her view, she kept on for a few seconds before slowing to a stop. Peering back, she pulled her hair free from the ribbon securing it high on her head, a tactic she used to keep it from obliterating her view as she cycled; a few scabby knees and bruised elbows helped her discover it. She tossed her head upside down and shook as hard as she could, two hands scratching at her scalp to rid it of any mites before pulling it back into position, this time wrapping it around itself to save it from catching on any branches as she passed through. She shivered. It was colder, no doubt from the lack of light, she told herself, easing back onto the seat and beginning to pedal. That's all it was; lack of light. It was dark too, exceptionally so. There was still a breeze despite the mass of trees, forcing a layer of goosebumps to surface as she made her way through the thick of it toward the village. The colour of the leaves caught her eye, they were beautiful – oranges, reds, gold – their colour seeping up through the ground as she stared toward her front wheel. She noticed for the first time what she was doing. She wasn't her usual gay self, looking at the beauty around her, she was nervous, staring at the ground to distract herself from her surroundings. Stupid, she thought, glancing up and peering around. It was the same as ever: trees. She told herself to snap out of it but she couldn't, the fear was pushing her feet harder into the pedals, forcing her legs down and her bum up off the seat. The branches above her swayed in the breeze, creaking in complaint. It was haunting, like some far-off cry. She hated it, she wished she'd stayed on the path and taken the long way round. What was it they were saying, that Polly and some others were found here, or went missing here? What about Mathew and Jodie? The colours of the leaves merged into one long streak as she charged over them in an attempt to broach the edge; she decided it didn't matter where it took her out, so long as she was out. The autumn light was cutting through the trees far ahead of her, illuminating the swarm it harboured. She sighed in relief; eating a few more midges meant nothing, she would just be glad to be out of there.

The hum grew louder as she neared the edge. She had noticed it a moment or so ago but couldn't see clearly what was making it. She had guessed, though, what it might be. She wouldn't have known, wouldn't have had a clue except she had heard them talking of the moths that cluster in places. Trust this to be one of them. Moths were lovely, like large, dark butterflies, Howard said, and he was right, they were, when there were one or two of them. Not like here. She slowed, stunned by the sight. The air was thick with them, dappled light dancing around their wings as they moved. She hesitated, considering whether to continue on and try further down or just cycle right through them and be out the other side. That was best, right?

Head down, eyes closed, she charged through them like a bull in the field charging a flag-waving man. Him against it, survival of the fittest. The cold air hit her face with a burn as she burst out the other side. Freedom, she thought, opening her eyes to see Black Water Lake. She pulled on the breaks and looked back. It wasn't like her to be so silly, she thought. Imagine being scared of the wood.

The sun shone down through the cold, it was warm on her face as she turned it up to the light but the darkness caught her eye. Even then it wasn't pleasant, not anymore, not even from here. She cycled on.

The bell above the door of Sparkle and Spools rang as Lilly entered, her bicycle propped against the wall outside. She had three things on her list: medium-width black thread, patch material and twine. The twine had nothing to do with the mending; it was for another purpose altogether.

'Hello Miss Lilly, you know what you're after okay?' enquired Mrs Spool politely. They knew one another well but she still did her the courtesy of offering her help, even at the risk of seeming a menace.

'Yes, thank you, I'll just be a second,' smiled Lilly.

There were two others in the shop, one she recognised as Tommy Tinkit and an older girl she assumed to be his sister; she remembered her face from the funeral. They stood huddled together like a pair of abandoned cubs.

The bell above the door rang. Margaret bustled in, sweeping a few stray hairs free from her mouth.

'Awful breeze out there, just awful. Oh hello, Lilly,' she cooed, catching sight of her sorting through the spools of thread to the back of the shop.

Lilly hadn't looked to see who had entered. She hadn't needed to; she knew by the bustling who it must be.

'Oh Lilly, I'm sorry if we shocked you the other day with all that talk of the wood and the goings on. I had no idea you hadn't heard it before. It's such old news to us Thatchies. Anywho, I just assumed . . .'

Lilly turned with a smile, 'Don't be silly, I'm glad to know, can't believe I had never heard any of it myself. Think Howard tried to keep it from me as best he could —'

Margaret cut her dead. 'He must be livid with me, letting it all out like that about Mrs Christmas Eve and . . .' She stuttered for a moment in an exaggerated pause, lowering her voice to a loud attempt at a whisper. 'It was the wood you know, got Charlie. It's like we were saying, you pay dearie, you definitely pay for what you've done and not in the Christian sense neither.'

'Well if anyone knows the ways of the land around here it's Howard,' Mrs Spool interjected, her head peering out from behind Suzie's. 'They've been there a long time, the questions,' she said, nodding toward the door and Thickets Wood. 'New happenings just rouse its head.'

Tommy stood closer to Suzie, his hands deep in his pockets. She was hard to ignore, Miss Margaret. He hadn't meant to listen, hadn't wanted to hear what she had said, but there was no avoiding it. He turned toward the door and pulled hard on the handle,

Rebecca Reid

the bell ringing as it flailed open, crashing to a stop against a row of material as he bolted out.

Margaret stood open-mouthed, stunned at the ruckus. 'Poor boy,' she sighed with a shake of her head, her glance falling to Suzie frantically paying for her things and stuffing them into her bag, half running, half fumbling as she hurried after him. 'Poor family,' she added.

There was a temporary silence.

'Howard's not annoyed in the slightest, it just never came up and he wasn't going to bring it up. One of those unsaid things,' Lilly continued, having gathered her thoughts back to their prior conversation.

9.

'I know this is difficult.'

She's rubbing her eyes.

She's started doing that, when she reaches something she really doesn't want to see. It seems to block it out.

Forcing her knuckles in deeper, as deep as they can go into the sockets – the swirls appear. All black, white and greys. They ache, a low, humming sort of ache. It's soothing. A distraction. Your mind can go nowhere else while it's here.

She's distracted by another ache. She needs to pee. She stops rubbing and wonders how long she's been holding it. By the intensity, she imagines a while. Sliding from beneath the cot, she ambles toward the changing wall. The ground is warm against her foot. The change in temperature forces her arm closer to her crotch in an attempt to prolong her hold. She pauses. Staring. It is separated, cut off from the room like a little box. She didn't like that a first, it was too small, confined, despite being able to see out. It's different now; she quite likes the privacy. Whipping her pants down, she collapses onto the bowl. Relief. That's another good thing: there is no need for balance. In the other room, her room, the bucket topples if she isn't careful. Then she has wee on her feet. She hates that. But not here.

She's not dimwitted, she does remember a toilet. She had one with *him*, initially. That was before.

'Come in, come in,' was the first she heard of his voice. It was hurried, flustered. They were outside, they had to be because he freed her from the boot and the shock of cold air was like her first breath. She was walking; she remembers a grip on her arm dragging her blindly before they hit a door that led inside. It squeaked on its hinges – that would come to mean a lot to her, but for now, it was nothing more than a squeaky door.

'You have her bagged, my beautiful Julia? You have her bagged.'

Who was Julia? She wasn't. Were there two of them? Was there another?

The light shocked her, she could see nothing at first, it took all her worth to blink away the tears brought on by the contrast. She hadn't noticed how well she had adapted to the dark. This boded well for her future, she knews that now.

There were two of them, standing, leering at her like some prize they won in a raffle, deciding whether to bother taking it home or not. One she knew, the other, the other was him.

He's . . .

She's beginning to fight it, the cold burn of the ceramic wrapping its way around her thighs. She peels them free, still sitting, just rocking gently – back and forth, back and forth.

She knows she has to.

They've told her it's time.

He's . . .

He's tall. Not terribly tall for a man, not small either, just average. From what she knew, she was nine. Anything looks tall when you're nine. The brown of his hair is dashed with grey around his face, not throughout. It's short and dull, no shine, just lifeless in *appearance. Much like his skin. It seemed grey. His eyes are green, like a marble, green with grey swirled in. He's not old, maybe forty. She couldn't tell, not properly. He was older than the other guy, she knew that much.*

'Hello Julia,' he said, a smile spreading across his face so large she saw the gold at the back of his mouth.

He sank backward onto a chair, never shifting his gaze, even as he raised a glass from the table. 'Well done John, meet my Julia.'

Who is Julia? Her name is Lilly.

Enough. That's enough.

There is an ache in her bottom from the pressure of the seat. She stands rubbing it. The rubbing helps. There's a flash in her mind – it's him. She bangs back in shock, her head hitting the support wall of the toilet. It doesn't hurt. She does it again, this time for effect; maybe she can shake him out. And again. And again.

She needs to be away, not from here, well yes, from here, from him, from the thought. She wants to run away.

★

The ground sent shocks to his knees with every pounding lunge, his feet moving hard and fast as he charged through the roads. He raced past Nik Naks, sending someone spinning as he flew past them. It was bad timing, they happened to grace the outer step just as he was cutting its corner. Bad luck. He wouldn't have stopped even if he had seen them; he may have swerved but it was too late, he clipped them and kept on going. The air was cold in his lungs, burning as he gasped it in at the top of the hill. He stopped, he had to, he'd run all the way through the village to the

Cauldwell place. He stood for a moment, his hand grasping the wire to steady him. There were tremors in his thighs and they hurt. Good God. A searing pain cut through his torso. He fell to the ground grasping his side as the pain shot through him like fire. He'd never felt anything like it. He thought for a moment he might be about to die. Unrealistic given it was in his lower side but he did, if even just for a second.

He wondered if his father had thought that. If he'd had time to wonder before it happened. Stan said he was drunk, but if he's wrong, if he wasn't, he may have wondered. Death, he thought, death mightn't be so bad. He'd thought about it a lot recently, what with his father passing. Death had a lot to say for itself with his family. The Tinkits were on his list, always had been. It would be of no surprise if he were next, not to him anyway. Perhaps not even to his mother. She was a slave to him anyway, he'd shaken her ragged and left her for dead years ago. Nothing shocked her now. Maybe a miracle, maybe that would. Would take one, he pondered now, stretching himself flat by the roadside, the pain beginning to ease enough to reassure him there was a little life left in him yet. Overall he was relieved but there was a small part of him that sighed in disdain. It meant more of the now and the now was far from pleasant or tolerable.

He lay, eyes closed, and listened for a moment. There was nothing but clucking coming from the winter hen coop. It was nice, reminded him of nature and the wildness of it, the unpredictability. He was envious for a moment, envious of their freedom. Well, not the Cauldwell chickens, they weren't entirely free, but nature, nature's freedom. Opening his eyes, he stared up at the greying sky above him, taking in the heavy, bouldering clouds that hung back, deep-set in the weight of everything around them. Their darkness was reminiscent of everything in his life right now. He hoped they would open up and rain, he wished for it. Rain would wash everything away. Clean it at least, clean out all the crap.

He gave it three minutes then got bored waiting and pushed himself to his feet, rubbing any clinging debris free before hoofing it home. He was hoofing it home because of the one thing he hadn't thought about laying there, the one thing he didn't want to think about. What he'd heard, what Miss Margaret was saying. He didn't even want to think it now, not out here all exposed. He could feel it, heavy and dark, running alongside him as he bound through the field that ran up to his house. It ran when he ran, it went where he went. He knew that, he had known it before now.

He paused at the fence running around their patch and looked at what was familiar, what was his. The house was white, washed in some natural thing his pa had brought back from a job well before he was born. It was pleasant to look at. It was low-rise, no stairs or second floor for them. Handy, he thought now, given the drink; stairs may have taken him away far sooner. A smile crept onto his lips, it was perhaps sadistic to laugh at that, given the circumstance, but he truly knew if he didn't, he would cry. That was another thing he had been doing a lot of recently.

The front door wasn't central as you would expect but to the far right, with only one set of windows beside it before you broached the edge. That was the sitting room. Pa had chosen to leave that, preserved, as it were, a little patch of the past in the jigsaw of their house. He had liked how it was untouched, said he could feel the people in it, their lives through all the years. He thought it not right to take away all the memories from a place by changing it all. That's why he built to the left. There were three sets of windows to the left. The first used to be a play area, it now served as an extra living room. His father spent a lot of his evenings there before he passed, if his wife was up; it was simpler that way. Tommy had noticed, they all had but they chose not to mention it, leave it as a peacemaker that deep down they all appreciated.

The other two windows were bedrooms, first Suzie's, then Tommy's. He couldn't see it from where he was standing, but toward the back were four more, Ethan's, Stan's, his parents and baby Lila's. Lila's was the furthermost; it had been built last and lay dormant at the back of the house. He never went down that far, none of them did. His father had wanted to change things, knock it through and make it another bathroom or a larger bedroom for themselves but his mother wasn't having any of it, she wasn't even hearing it.

'You could do that couldn't you? Just crash right through it with a hammer like she was never there. Well she was and she always will be!'

That was all that was ever said of the matter. From then on, it lay empty. Untouched.

The dogs were barking, breaking his thoughts. He could see them now, all seven of them battering against one another to charge him. They were in a large pen, off to the right and set back a bit. He and his brothers helped knock it together a few years ago when the numbers were growing and keeping track of them was becoming a bit of a chore. It was mainly wire roll and wood but there were patches of netting and slabs of metal and stone here and there where they had chewed their way out to chase after things at night. Shadow was the worst, she was a digger; hell to keep in. A lot of their time is spent loose but when the family are heading out it's safest to put them away, keep them out of trouble; wouldn't want any of them getting shot or snared.

Snares are the worst. It had only happened the once but Stan said at the time he thought it was the main reason his pa had gone about building the pen. It was Willy; he was one of the younger wild ones his father had brought home. He did that, that's where the majority of them came from, the wild. Willy had been running loose miles away near Potter's Cove, a lake used for the seasonal fishing. Rolf Tinkit would stay up there for a few days at a time, catch what he could, then sell what he brought back to the locals. This would go on for a month or so, to-ing and fro-ing, living in his beat-up truck and dining on boiled rice; he couldn't afford to eat any of his catch. Mind you, this particular year he made the exception of the odd one for the wild dog he'd been befriending – Willy. He wasn't the nervous type, not like some Rolf had worked with in the past; had him convinced he wasn't wild blood through and through. No, Willy was the opposite. He'd run with anybody who'd have him, and Rolf would have him.

He was with them a year before it happened, long enough for everyone, including his mother, to fall in love with him. Willy was all about life; he saw fun in everything, to the point of utter destruction. This particular day it was leaping through Farmer Rose's cabbage field. They heard the howls as far away as the village. It was the worst sound Tommy had ever heard, or ever would, he imagined – the howls and the yelping when they got there. They saw the snare before they saw Willy.

'Get my gun from the back,' Rolf said with a sigh. 'Get it!' he snapped, unnerved at the prospect of what was ahead. Tommy didn't understand why he had to get the gun. He did soon enough. The worst of it was the hope in his eyes when he saw his father coming. He calmed, it was beautiful to see. Tommy was sent to wait in the truck; he only saw from afar. The gun fell to the ground, still smoking hot as he ran to him. He had never seen his father cry, not since Lila, not once, but the tears were there when he came back, Willy, snare and all, in his arms. His blood-sodden shirt draped over the worst of it to protect not just Tommy, but himself. It was too painful to see, even for a fully grown man. Love is love, doesn't matter who or what, it still hurts just the same, Tommy learnt that day. A lesson he'll never forget. It takes a man to be one and it takes a man to be honest enough to show he's more than one. He saw his father differently that day, he saw him from afar, he saw him as a man. Not his father, just a man.

They didn't drive home as he had expected, instead they drove to the Rose family home. Tommy was told to stay in the truck but he saw it in the rear view, he saw him punch him, he saw him rubbing his fist as he got back into the truck and the red coming up on his knuckles as they dug the hole to put him in out back.

'Could have been one of you kids,' he said, tugging the bottle free from his boot and resting on the spade while he took a glug. Tommy stood stunned; he had thought it was all about Willy.

They continued to bark as he untied the door and swung it free. He controlled them as his father had before letting them loose, that way they would listen to him and come back, or so he hoped. So he'd been taught anyway.

The air was warm as he opened the door to the cottage and stepped inside. It surprised him; he had forgotten they had lit the fires before they left for the shop. He hadn't just forgotten that, he had forgotten Suzie too. There was a twang of guilt as he remembered how she had run after him, calling.

The hallway was dark leading to the kitchen, it was boxed in with no natural light except what little crept through from the gap in the wall ahead. He paused at the spot it had happened and wondered for a second if it felt the same. It did. Strange how a place can absorb an incident and be none the wiser; he wished people could be the same, be a lot easier that way. The exact spot felt no different, but the house did. It did to him anyway, he wasn't sure about the others. He hadn't asked them, nor did he intend to, but to him it felt different, that's all that mattered. Hearing what they had to say on the matter wasn't going to change that. There was a weight in the heat of the room, an empty weight. It wasn't just in the heat, he felt it in the cold too, and not just here – everywhere, the whole house, his whole life even. He paused and wondered if that was it, if it was nothing to do with the place and it was to do with him, all of it.

The kitchen was relatively tidy except for the bread knife sitting surrounded by crumbs – she had been up, his mother. The logs he had stacked earlier that morning had diminished somewhat, she must have kept the fires going. He had wondered how they lasted so long unattended. He smiled, it pleased him that she cared enough. He lifted a log now and tossed it in. There was a crackle as it caught alight, the flame drawing him in, causing him to stare, unblinking; there was a comfort in it. The house was still and quiet except for the echo of barking coming from all around. They were frolicking in the field, he assumed; it was their favourite pastime.

As he stepped forward to glace out the window, the feeling came back, the guilt he had so easily repressed earlier, but this guilt wouldn't go away, not so easily, it never had. There were levels of guilt, he had decided that years ago, and this level didn't shake easily. He watched as they charged around the field, he watched as they broached the edge and then a new feeling crept in, one less lived-in – fear. Their cottage sat right on the edge of Thickets Wood.

10.

I don't like it there. I don't like it. It's dark, darker than it used to be.

She's resting her elbows on the cot. It's different. She bolts upright, shocked. The mattress is thick and bouncy. It's new. The bedding is clean and white, not crisp but soft. She fumbles for her sheet; it's on her knee. She sighs, relieved. She knows where she is; she's in the changing room. This isn't her cot, it's theirs. She hesitates. They're here, she can feel it, they are always here. Even at night if ever she comes in, they're here.

She's becoming intrigued.

She wants to see them but she doesn't want to look, not directly anyway. She turns slightly, her view toward the toilet wall, and curls down toward her knees, slowly, pulling her sheet close to her face in the process. She can see them, they're there. One is watching her, not intensely but with a gentle ease. She's seen enough. She sinks lower and creeps beneath the cot. She doesn't want to be looked at. She lies, her back hard against the wall, the sheet draped from her head to her toes, her knees tight against her chest. She can see them but they can't see her. It's safe.

'I want you to meet the family,' he said smiling, again the gold of his teeth catching her eye. 'But not yet, you're not ready. Do you like "Julia"? Do you mind? It's what I'd really like to call you.'

He seemed nice. It wasn't the worst thing to agree to, she thought with a shrug, but he had already turned away. It hadn't been a question, she realised – more of a polite statement. She was standing in a kitchen. It was roomy, slightly worn, she thought, noticing the odd crooked door and battered corner. The fridge caught her eye; there were pictures on it, not photographs but drawings and paintings; they were old, favourites, she thought, by the browning of the paper. Children's. Children's! He might have kids. This could be okay.

'I noticed you're dark.' He hesitated. 'No. I was told you were.' He held a box in his hand. She wondered what it was, looking at the pretty lady on the front with long blonde hair. It meant nothing to her. 'We'll sort that out, come with me.'

There was a door off the kitchen with a frosted glass top, it was a bathroom. She was beginning to feel uneasy; it didn't seem right being in the bathroom with a man she didn't know.

'I thought it would be fun, see what it's like,' he grinned, sensing her apprehension, 'bit like playing dress-up. Do you want to play?'

She nodded, unsure what he meant. Then he told her to kneel in front of the bath so he could wash her hair. It felt a bit strange at first; she had been washing her own hair for years now, but he was gentle and it was harmless. The shampoo made her eyes sting. She squeezed them shut and said something, she doesn't remember his reply, she simply remembers him wrapping her hair in a towel and making her sit before he 'rinsed' it. They played 'I spy'. He was rather good, but she was better. He noted the colour of her eyes saying they were paler but 'would do'. It was strange but she thought nothing much of it at the time. After her hair was rinsed he pointed out the clothes on the stool. She had seen them when they first came in but now he was drawing her attention to them.

'I hope they fit,' he said, a patter of excitement in his voice. 'You look much better already,' he added.

He closed the door as he left. She was glad, she had thought for a moment that he might stay and watch while she changed. They were far from new: well-washed, she thought, by the faded colour and well-worn from the bobbles roughed-up on the cotton. Looking at the labels, they read 'Ages 7-8'. She was nine. She put them on all the same. She was only new after all, it seemed polite. They were slightly small. The leggings came halfway up her calf, and the T-shirt and cardigan sat at her waist and a good bit up her forearm. He didn't seem to mind.

'Julia,' he said, hugging her.

A strand of her hair caught above his shoulder in the hug – it was pale. Yellow. She eased back on his release and pulled a clump around to look at it. It was blonde. He had dyed her hair blonde.

'Do you like it? I told you dress-up was fun.'

She stood silenced. It hadn't been a question; she had learnt that from the first time.

She puts her hand to it now. It's heavy. Lank. She doesn't remember it any other way, not clearly. Then there's the itch. Always the itch. She scratches, one hand at first, then the other. Relief.

He used to do it, before. He was the last to do it. Rinsing it with the empty bottle he kept in the bath. It was how he always did it, he said, with her.

She's scratching harder, deeper with her nails.

'Dirty. Dirty.'

She's becoming frantic.

'Calm.'

She jumps.

A voice. She heard it, she definitely heard it. They spoke.

She drops her hands to the sheet and yanks it over her head. Her feet are exposed. Normally this would bother her but not now, now it's the last thing she's thinking about.

Somewhere else. Not here. The itch, she recalls, what itch? She relaxes the tension in her neck and rests her cheek on the warm of the floor. Somewhere else, she thinks, closing her eyes. Somewhere else.

★

Lilly woke to the sound of rain crashing on the outhouse roof. It was a drumming, an incessant drumming. She rolled her eyes wearily, wondering when Howard would find the time to fix it properly. The metal was a temporary measure to keep the water from getting in.

'There's no wood the right size. I'm going to have to use this strip of tin for now, just until I get around to sorting it out properly,' he'd said.

That was four days ago.

She drew back the curtain and peered out. It was as she expected, grey and miserable. Typical.

'Back to bed with you. I'll be there in a second.'

She had hoped for as much, smiling from cheek to cheek as she sprang back into bed and yanked at the covers. There were three layers on the bed at this time of year: a duvet, a throw, and a bigger, heavier quilt that had been in the family since Howard's grandmother's day. Come a month from now she would add the second duvet. She liked to be warm when she slept, much to Howard's dismay; he slept sprawled out with all but the throw tossed to the side.

'Hope you're in there,' he called from the stairs.

'Yep,' she said, scrabbling for the third layer.

Howard eased the door open with the toe of his boot, the tray appearing through the opening before he did. She smiled. He hadn't forgotten. He never had before and she assumed he never would, but there's always that little niggle of fear that one year he might miss it by a day or so. It was silly; she should know him better than that by now.

'Happy birthday Lilly,' he beamed, resting the tray on her ready-smoothed lap.

The smell had hit her as she looked out the window, she knew what to expect and she was right: eggs, two to be exact, bacon, and something she hadn't expected – eggy toast. She adored eggy toast. On the side was a glass of freshly squeezed juice, a jug of syrup and a flower made out of paper.

'Know how much you love them,' he smiled, following her stare. 'Not much in the garden for picking this time of year and sorry to say there's not much of an artist in me even if I am good with these hands.'

He was right, it wasn't a brilliant example of a daisy but it was a beautiful attempt with its rough-cut leaves and twig stem. It was the highlight of her day, he just didn't know it.

'I'm going to get that leak fixed first thing,' he said, wandering toward the window and peeking out to trace the sound. 'You going to Rabbit's Burrow this morning, meet the ladies?'

She swallowed down a mouthful before answering, 'Yes, eleven o'clock. What time is it?'

'Bought eight-twenty, thereabouts.'

She giggled. 'Bit of a lie in.'

'Aw, deep down you knew it was a big day ahead.'

His eyes were warm, tender in the curve that drew them up from his smile. He adored her.

'Twenty-four,' he grinned, shaking his head. They had been together as long as they'd been apart. 'Hard to believe,' he added, his weight heavy on the pane as he leant against it.

'Do you mind?' he queried, a quick flick of his finger to his shirt pocket, the cigarette appearing, just visible above the cut of blue cotton. 'I'll open the window a little,' he added, his nudge of encouragement; he could tell she was hesitating.

She stalled, contemplating her options and wondering which would be worse. She was going to let him smoke; she knew that much already, it was just weighing up the negatives between a smoky room or a cold room. She decided smoky was the lesser of the two evils and suggested he use the now-empty jug as an ash-tray. He hated having to do that, it seemed disrespectful, but there was no alternative. The match sizzled as he struck it, the searing noise it made enhanced as he drew on the cigarette to get it to take. It was his first smoke of the day and it felt good. He watched Lilly watch him, she didn't like the smell, didn't like any-thing about it but she liked the habit. She liked that the musky smell of smoke and aftershave wafted around her when he entered a room, she liked when a cigarette hung from his bottom lip as he sat quietly thinking. He was doing it now, thinking, the butt sticking to his lip, hanging gently, just tipping into his mouth on command, then resting back with the weight of the ash pulling it down. She liked the silences they shared, they both did.

'A sign of contentment Lou, having the confidence to sit in silence in company, a sign of understanding,' he'd say. Nothing could be more true, not if they were anything to go by.

He watched her now, finishing up her toast and thought about the day she came to be with him. He didn't often think about it, it ached him to do so, but every now and then, usually at a time like this, it would just come to him and he thanked the Lord for her and everything He'd given them together.

She'd said she was nine, the wee thing, she was far from it,

Rebecca Reid

perhaps even older than eleven but it seemed a fair enough guess at the time. She was a scrap of the woman she is now, a waif, a tortured soul. You wouldn't know it, he thought, the ash crashing off the lip of the jug as he flicked it. Lilly hadn't noticed; he rubbed any debris into the ground with his boot, being sure to double-check it hadn't left a mark – it hadn't, not really, not a significant one. It was a learning curve for him too, having to learn about young ladies so fast, how to deal with them at the best of times was a handful, never mind this scenario. He was like a drowning man the first few months. He stifled a laugh; it was more like the first year or so.

'What's so funny?'

Damn, she had noticed. He wasn't going to tell her the truth, not have it be reared up again; he had to think on his feet.

'Just thinking over how I made a botch of the first few eggs I did this morning.'

Not bad for an old fool, he thought.

She set down the cutlery and stretched. It had been a lovely breakfast and now she was ready for her shower. Howard put his boot over the slight smudge on the ground as she rose. He thought she hadn't noticed. She had. This made her smile; he knew her so well. It was hard for her to let him smoke indoors at the best of times, never mind when he goes dropping ash everywhere.

'Happy birthday Lou,' he said as she wrapped her arms around his waist and rested her head on the warm of his shirt. 'Here's to another great year.'

'If you get that roof fixed it will be,' she jested, jumping back and dashing from arm's-length as he sought something to swipe at her.

'Any more of that and this year the picnic will be outside,' he called after her, a laugh in his voice as he picked up the tray and made his way back downstairs.

Lilly stayed at Rabbit's Burrow much longer than expected. They had an iced bun with a cherry on top waiting for her when she arrived. It was the first time they had done such a thing and it touched her. The morning chat was the usual, catching up on the goings-on in one another's lives over the past few weeks and of course the goings-on in others'.

'See the sign's up then?' Margaret exclaimed, overjoyed at being the first to mention it.

'What sign's this then?' asked Miss Petal.

'Bet I can guess,' added Mrs Spool. 'Whitehall Cottage?'

'It is not!' Mertle gasped. 'I had no idea she was leaving, has anyone spoken to her?'

'No and no one can. She's away to her mum's, must have come back sometime in between and gathered up their things because according to Mr Allen, the place is empty,' continued Margaret. 'I'd say that's it, wouldn't you?' she asked no one in particular. 'Anywho, you wouldn't catch me hanging about if my husband went missing in those woods yonder. No sir, no knowing what could happen next,' she said with a shiver, her cup chinking on the table as she set it down awaiting a refill.

'Now that's just speculation,' chirped Lilly. It was less of a statement and more of a question. 'Right?' she said, turning to Mrs Rose, now sitting quietly listening.

She jumped slightly, having been in a daze. 'Yes, that's right, speculation, that's all it is —'

'All it ever is,' interrupted Mrs Spool, 'but more often than not that sort of thing's right.'

'I hate this talk of the woods, do we have to go over this again? Can we not just lay it to rest and move on?' said Miss Petal politely, a nervousness in her voice. 'There can't be any good in talking about it, we aren't ever going to understand.'

'Huh!' hooted Margaret. 'Understand? The only thing we need to understand is to be good-living and we're sure to be all right. I don't know about you lot but I get to sleep in my bed at night, even with all the goings-on, the whisperings about the what-ifs.'

'Same here,' added Mertle. 'Talking of all that, I went by the memory tree the other day to see if anything had been done about Charlie's —'

'But he's not necessarily dead?' queried Lilly, confused as to why anyone would be mentioning the memory tree. It was for births, deaths and marriages.

'Either way, he's not coming back. I just thought it right, in case, well, in case he is dead, I thought he ought to be on the tree, where he belongs,' finished Mertle, swishing a mouthful of coffee around her mouth to shut herself up.

Lilly shrugged in agreement, as did the rest of the group. It seemed like a nice idea, in case it were true, what everyone was thinking, even those not saying it.

Lilly lay, legs strung over the bottom of the bed, feet bumping a tune on the wood as they swung. She was becoming impatient. Howard was taking his time about calling her and she was sure her stomach was going to rumble any second. There it goes, she thought as her stomach let out a roar, and there I was thinking starvation was a thing of my past, she giggled to herself. She paused for a second and pushed herself up on her elbows. Had she just made a joke about it and laughed? She had and she couldn't quite believe it. She so wanted to dash downstairs and tell Howard but something stopped her, she didn't want to remind him, he had taken her so far from her past that she didn't want to bring him back there, especially not today. She dropped back down and remembered her first birthday with Howard, her twelfth. She had been blonde, even then. More than a year she'd been here and it was still growing out.

'With every bit of dark you see, you'll feel that little bit freer,' Howard had said. He'd reached out to touch her but reeled his hand back in; she wouldn't be ready, not yet. She remembers because part of her wanted him to, even though she recoiled. That was habit more than fear, but he had tried and that was nice. He'd been right not to cut it all off there and then when she begged. Right to make her watch the progress, see it slip away and the new, pure hair grow. It did feel a little better each time she noticed it. It cleansed her, like the dark was creeping out slowly. They kept the bottom trimmed, cutting off a bit every few months so the yellow was becoming less and less. It was all part of the process: out with the old, in with the new. It was hard, hard for both of them; she can see that now, looking back. He let her deal with things her way; whatever she wanted he let her do but once things were better, once she was better, he put a stop to any remembering. Not for him but for her. Said it was more than reminiscing, it was dredging up the past,

'It does no good to be raking over these things. Best to let the good in life wash over them, Lou.' He was right, she thought, stamping on the habit. She twisted a strand of long dark hair around her finger where she lay and drew her gaze from it to the ceiling. She couldn't have been happier.

'Lilly Lou,' Howard called from downstairs. Well maybe she

could, she thought, jumping to her feet and racing down to the sitting room.

There by the fire was the rug, all laid out with bowls, spoons and mugs. She couldn't wait, she knew what was ahead. The pot of hot chocolate hung boiling over the flame, a pot rested beside it and the smell of apple pie glided in from the oven.

'Stew,' he smiled, slipping a ladle into the pot. 'Then chocolate and apple pie,' he added with a twinkle in his eye. They had been having that for the past twelve years, since that very first birthday picnic. It meant something; it was special. He hoped they'd be doing it forever. At least, until his last days. She sat before him, cross-legged, rocking with excitement as she did the very first year.

Oh, how he adored her.

11.

She's shaking her head. She doesn't like it being in there. Not now. She'd kept it away for so long. See. See, she knew thinking back could do no good. See what it's done, what he's done. It's gone and moved in there. It's hers, all hers and hers alone. There. None of him. None of that.

She crawls out from beneath the cot and scuttles up onto its surface. She doesn't want them to . . . where are they?

She glances quickly around and sees the room empty. For a moment she's frightened. Change. She doesn't like change. But she doesn't like them, not here, not always. She realises then that she's in here more than there. She likes the warmth. The light. The things she had hated about it she now likes.

She begins to panic. So much change, in there and out here. She is gripping her head in her hands, rocking.

In there, she thinks. Patting her hands either side of her head. In there.

It doesn't hurt to rock. The mattress is thick and spongy. It's everywhere, she thinks, becoming frenzied. Change. How can she like it? The concept confuses her. She's banging harder on her head. He did this, he did it.

'We'll meet them in the morning. It's late for them and you,' he said, placing an arm around her shoulders and steering her along the

hallway and up the stairs to a closed door. It was white, painted and glossy, like any other, until he opened it. She couldn't believe it, it was better than at her grandparents'. The walls were pink, with yellow skirts, the curtains striped in pastels, matching the duvet cover on the bed. There were toys, books, dolls. It was a perfect room for a little girl. He had gone to so much trouble. She turned to him and smiled, it was the first genuine smile she'd given him since they'd met earlier that evening. He must really want her, she thought, to get everything so perfect, so right.

'You're home,' he grinned.

It felt strange, him saying that, 'home'. It wasn't her home but, she hesitated in thought, it was meant to be, from now on, this was meant to be. She couldn't grasp it for a moment. It seemed too far-fetched that she had gone from her grandfather's lap to this.

She felt a nudge in her back. He was pushing her inward, over the step of the door and into the room.

'It's late. The pyjamas are under your pillow as usual. I'll come for you in the morning to meet the others,' he said, stressing the words to make a point. What point, she wasn't sure. She nodded, smiling as he closed the door.

The room smelt of newly sprayed polish, fresh and cleaned. It was only when she went to lift the toys that the stuffiness entered the room. The books felt old, musty. They weren't new, or even newly placed. They had been there a while, a long while she imagined. The wardrobe stood tall in the far corner of the room from the bed. She bit her lip and wondered if it was full of nice new clothes for her, or empty waiting to be filled. The suspense was too much, she crept over and strained to reach the handle. It was too high. Then she spied the chair by the table. Dragging it over, she set it close to the door but with enough room for her to yank it open and not topple herself off. She managed it, just. Inside were none of the things she had contemplated. There were no new clothes, it was not empty, it was full to the brim with worn, used clothes. She rummaged through. It was all the same, as were the ages, meaning he would have to take her shopping for something new that would fit. She couldn't go anywhere for long wearing clothes this small.

Morning came and she opened the bedroom door into the hall hoping to hear some commotion, children getting up, raking around as she would some days, but nothing. Her toe broached the step when he appeared looming over her.

'Get in,' he demanded harshly. He noticed her reaction, drawing attention to his tone and tried hard to appear friendly. 'I told you I would come for you, I always come for you,' he said, pulling the door closed as she backed away.

Always. Always, she thought, over and over as she sat on the bed still in the too-small pyjamas, unsure what to do next, get dressed, stay the same, what would he want?

He came, eventually, and led her by the hand, down the stairs and into the kitchen to meet the family.

The family, she thought, open-mouthed.

Her mouth is open now. She can see it and doesn't like it, the memory. She is still rocking but the patting has stopped. She thinks perhaps they stopped her. She can't remember, she was somewhere else. Somewhere dark. She settles herself and rolls onto her side facing the wall, close enough to it that she can feel the roughness graze her nose. It's time for something nice. Enough of that, before, got to focus on something nice. She knows what she wants. She's searching for them . . .

★

117

The noise of clattering woke him. It hadn't been much of a sleep anyway, he'd been restless, jumpy. This was a new thing; he had always been such a good sleeper before. He stretched until his shoulders cracked, recalling his dream and jumping free from it and his bed onto the cold wooden floor. It hadn't been pleasant and he would rather shake the feeling it had cast over him now than live in its shadow for the day, something he was getting used to; it was becoming the norm. He could hear Sally through the window. It was Tuesday, his day to milk her. He sighed at the prospect, not because he disliked it, but because it left him alone to think for too long. Still, at least he only did it once a week; it was one of the privileges of being the youngest. The trail of noise led to the kitchen where Suzie was busy getting everyone rallied together for school.

'Stan, enough of that,' she said crossly, snatching the bag of cereal from his hand and slamming it on the counter. 'You're supposed to be helping me, now set the table and don't eat anything until we're all around it! Tommy,' she said, exasperated, 'you were meant to be up early this morning, get Sally milked before breakfast.' She looked at him with disappointment. 'Well?'

Well what? he thought, smart enough not to say it out loud given the mood she was in. 'I had a terrible night, otherwise I would have been up —'

'Right, well out you go and get it done while I get things together in here. Ethan, you can help him.'

Ethan looked up from the bag he was packing for school and groaned. He was cut short with a glare; he chose to file in as commanded rather than argue. He looked at her creased brows and tight mouth. No, today was not the day to argue. After all, Sally was only there because of him.

Sally and Jess lived in a pen just to the back of the garden, beyond the kitchen. They were pets of necessity rather than pleasure but they kept them well all the same with a nice wooden shelter built on the edge of the old well. The well wasn't in working order, hadn't been since long before they moved there. Rolf had intended to get it cleared out and running again, but that day would never come; they all realised that now. Individually, at one time or another over the past few weeks, they had come to see it. The milking pad stood at the far end of the pen. It was a makeshift wooden frame with a raised platform, a foot or so off the ground, and a tall back with a feeding gap in the middle for the girls to lean through while they were being milked.

Mrs Tinkit had seen to it that they got the goats when Ethan was a toddler and his skin started acting up. It took her a few months of trial and error with numerous things before she realised what was making him itch: it was milk, cow's milk. There was no alternative but to get the girls and learn how to milk them. She had Mr Tinkit build the pen and then she went about teaching herself what needed to be done. She couldn't and wouldn't have one of her little'ens suffering from ingesting the wrong stuff or being deprived of milk either. The family were summoned, young as they were, and each learnt how to do their bit. At first it was no more than feed them and clean them out, then they learnt how to coax them up on the pad and so on until they got where they are now, each taking their turn. Milking in winter is harder, harder to warm them up enough to get the letdown, but once it's flowing pails fill up quickly enough. By the time they're finished Suzie and Stan have the fires lit, beds made, lunches ready and breakfast on the table. Tommy thinks that perhaps he got off lightly today; he had company so there was no time to get lost in thought and it got him off the indoor chores.

'What you smiling at?' asked Suzie, a hand outstretched for the milk, the other offering a plate of toasted bread for the table.

'Was I? Didn't realise,' he replied snapping out of it, noticing he had little time to eat and get to school.

'Toast and cereals there boys, I'm taking Ma her tea and I'll be back,' she said, resting the milk by the door and lifting the waiting tray. 'Leave me some!' she bellowed from the hallway. She knew better than to leave a table full of food and not say so; it would result in a certain handful of pitiful faces claiming they thought she had eaten. That was their usual point of argument. They were growing boys, she knew what that meant, more so now than ever, now that her mother had been bedridden for over a month and her father was no longer around. It made her realise how much he had done despite his apparent absence.

The walk to her mother's room felt cold and empty. It was a combination of the stone floor and the lack of tread in that direction; the boys seldom visited her when she was laid up and she seldom ventured this way except to go to the bathroom. She knocked the door, pausing to wait for approval before walking on in; it was only polite, even if it was her mother. Today though, there was no call of 'okay'. Instead, the door flew open and an already dressed Mrs Tinkit stood before her.

'Suzie my lovely,' she said with a smile, her hand caressing beneath her daughter's chin. 'I thought I'd try and get up today, have breakfast with the boys before they head to school. Took me a little longer to get myself gathered together than I thought, am I too late?' she queried, disappointment creeping over her face.

'No, not at all. Well, not if we're quick. You know how they wolf everything down,' she smiled, fighting to contain her excitement. She had thought that was it, perhaps the grief had been the last straw and she would never recover, seems she had been wrong – and nothing could make her happier.

The boys took little notice of their mother entering the room. Nor did they care much when she joined them at the table. It meant less food, that was as far as their thoughts took them. Well most of them, not Tommy. Tommy noticed. He noticed the burden of guilt lift off his shoulders, not entirely, but a little. It was lighter, he could breath more freely. He inhaled with a smile and sighed it out. If only she could get over his death. It was selfish really and he knew it, he cared little for his mother, emotionally. It was the causes of her weakness that concerned him and those concerns would be eliminated by her improvement – that was what he was seeking. Not a mother, he was doing fine without her, he had Suzie, but all the same, her improvement was important to him, even if it was for the wrong reasons.

Breakfast was late which meant they were, so they scrabbled for their coats and bags and dashed for the door on the trek to school. It wasn't far but lack of enthusiasm always made the journey more drawn-out than need be and lateness was frowned upon.

'Tommy,' his mother called as his foot broached the doorway.

'Yes,' he replied, watching as Ethan and Stan ran on ahead of him.

'Would you go into Nik Naks on your way home? Here's a list and the money. Get what you can,' she said, smiling as she placed them in his hand.

'Okay, bye,' he called, having stuffed them into his pocket as he charged after the others; he was at the gate when she said goodbye, but he couldn't hear her. She smiled; her family was doing brilliantly without him, just as she thought they would. A worthless drunk. A heartless, worthless drunk. It made her smile, made her happy knowing nobody missed him, knowing they were as self-sufficient as she had thought all these years. She believed it, truly believed it because they sheltered her from their emotions, protected her from their pain in the hope it would ease hers. How badly they misunderstood one another. How grossly they misread each others' signals for help.

Nik Naks stood on the corner of Chapel Road, named so after the church that took pride of place toward the top of the town. Tommy looked at it now, looming over everything, and thought of his father's funeral, thought of his father in general. He had never been much of a believer, like his mother; the Tinkits chose to have their children baptised but not to rear them with going to church, with the exception of Christmas. But they believed, Rolf at least; Mrs Tinkit lost her faith when Lila died, but Rolf, Rolf sought refuge in the belief that it was part of a plan, a plan that was bigger than him. She hated him for this too, hated that he had a way out of his grief that she didn't, a way that washed everything away, or so he made it appear. True, he washed it away, away in drink, Tommy thought now, staring at the building and hating it a little for confusing them. It wasn't a plan, he knew that. It wasn't God. It was nothing that could be explained away or prayed away. It had ruined everything: his mother, his father, his family. It had killed Pa and he would never forgive it. It wasn't the drink like everyone said, it was her.

'You coming in or you going to stand there in a daze all day?' Polly asked in a cheery tone from where she stood stacking apples into the outdoor baskets.

Tommy jumped.

'Didn't mean to startle you. Sorry,' she said slightly ashamedly. She knew he had been through a lot recently. She felt bad for him.

He smiled. 'It's okay, I was just thinking.'

'Well how are things? How's your mother?'

He smiled weakly. 'She's good, up this morning but I haven't seen her since.'

'It would be hard for her,' said Polly thoughtfully, 'losing your father so suddenly. I'm sure she's finding it tough. Give her my love,' she said, rubbing his shoulder tenderly as she passed on her retreat into the shop.

He followed close behind, pulling the crumpled list from his pocket and lifting a basket; they were handmade, wicker, produced for them by one of the locals. He wasn't sure who, he only noted it because of the weight – it always drew his attention.

The interior of Nik Naks was gloomy, though not for lack of windows; they had two large ones at the front but throughout autumn and winter the mass of produce seemed to absorb what little light there was and darken the place down. The shelves sat four tiers high, all wooden and painted, scruffy now with wear and tear but pleasant all the same.

'Oil, eggs, carrots, potatoes (ten) . . .' he muttered as he worked his way around the shop, inside and out. It went on to tell him to go to the bakery. She hadn't mentioned that, he assumed she had forgotten that it had been closed since Charlie had vanished a few months ago. He had told her; she mustn't have listened. He would have to get what he could from Rabbit's Burrow.

'I'm certain of it dearie, didn't Mertle tell you at the meeting? Oh I am surprised.'

It was Miss Margaret; he recognised the loud whisper coming from the back of the shop.

She stood crammed between the shelf laden with various forms of cabbage and something he couldn't quite make out; she was crammed between that and Miss Petal. It was an annex at the back, a kind of cove where the shop expanded down the side of the old storeroom. It was darker than the rest, cut off from any natural light by the box-like store cupboard.

'Just, Mrs Rose mentioned it. I hadn't thought of it myself but she was saying how, well we all know Charlie's guilty secret —'

Her voice became more hushed as she placed a hand discreetly over her mouth, watching for Polly as she wandered in and out of the shop door, unaware of Tommy loitering at a nearby shelf.

'We all know what he did, well most of us, and it makes sense, you know, what we were saying, that that was why she came —'

'Mrs Christmas Eve,' Miss Petal injected enthusiastically, sidling up closer so as to be sure not to offend Miss Polly.

'Yes, yes. That she came for him as comeuppance, make him pay for what he did. Well, she was saying it makes sense, what with the boy from the coop having vanished after he shot Miss Tiding, and Miss Tiding drowning in the river, for, well maybe we don't know what she had been and done to provoke it. See, it all adds up. All these things aren't so strange when you see them clearly.'

Miss Petal glanced around, seeing Tommy but not caring as she continued. 'And there were the others, years ago, before. Gosh,' this time, she mouthed the words rather than risk saying them, even in a whisper, 'Miss Polly.'

Tommy couldn't see so he didn't know who they were referring to any longer.

'What could she have done, do you think it was something —'

Margaret interrupted. 'Don't know, don't know but I think it makes sense. Makes sense of a lot of things.' She began to giggle, reaching out to touch Miss Petal's arm. 'Be hoping you have nothing dark in your past, Petal dearie. Hope none of us do.'

Miss Petal's face dropped. 'Guess we'll see, sooner maybe,

rather than later. She seems to be coming thick and fast if this last year's anything to go by.'

Tommy buckled at the stomach. He couldn't control it; it came over him like a convulsion. He gathered himself and stumbled toward the till. He couldn't do it, he felt dizzy, nauseous. He could taste it, the vomit in his mouth. He put the basket down by the till and apologised before stumbling out into the road.

'Are you okay?' Polly called after him.

He heard her, a distant voice as he ambled toward home, the list falling from his hand onto the dirt road. He didn't notice, he was numb.

12.

She raises herself onto her hand. Her arm had stuck to the sheet, she assumes it will be the same for her thigh. She peels it free and sits up, legs crossed. She's hot. Sticky all over. She thinks of in there, the cold cement floor. She feels the smile appear on her cheeks. It's heavy, she lets it go. The floor. She really wants the cold floor. The door is open, she can see the dark in comparison to out here. It used to close, the door in the changing wall. It never does now. She feels for the sheet on her lap, it's damp, sweat. She doesn't care. She swings it around her shoulders and slides free of the cot, darting toward the door. The darkness and cool both hit her at once. They seem strange. She realises it's been a while. They're nice. Soothing. She slides onto her knees, the grain scratching at her skin, and flops onto her back. She can do that here. Not in there with them, but here. They don't come in, not anymore; here she can be that free. Her fingers spread, the cool lacing around them like a well of blue she can see in her mind. She's used to that, seeing in her mind. It started long ago, it started with him.

The room was dark at first – not dark, gloomy. The curtains were drawn, making it hard to see anything beyond outlines. She could make out a table, the table he sat at last night, and people, two people. She felt nervous. He flicked on the light. 'Meet the family,' he said.

She stared in disbelief, speechless.

He prodded her shoulder. 'It's rude to stay silent.'

She glanced up at him, unsure of what to do next.

'Say hello,' he goaded, the kindness in his voice straining.

'Hello,' she stammered.

'This is Michelle,' he said moving around and placing his hands tentatively on the shoulders of the first inanimate doll, 'and this,' he said gesturing toward the other, 'well, this was my Julia before you came to join us. So let's call her Jay. We agreed on that last night didn't we pet?' He was speaking to the doll.

They were very different, Michelle and Jay. Michelle, the bigger of the two, was clearly a woman. She sat taller, and from what Lilly could see of her form in her silk nightie she had breasts, and her hair was long and pale brown. The other, Jay, was a child in every dimension. She had long blonde hair, blue eyes, and something Lilly had never seen before: a strip of metal across her teeth. She was a human-sized child doll.

She glanced repeatedly between the two, then up to him. His eyes met hers. He had been watching, judging how she perceived his family, her family. He wasn't well pleased for now.

'Breakfast,' he smiled, spinning toward the worktop. 'What'll it be?'

She stood in silence, surveying the situation. The table was set with four places; the dolls were at two, leaving one, she assumed, for herself, and the other for him.

'What'll it be?' he asked again. 'Toast or cereal? We're all out of porridge pet, but we do have cornflakes or there is always toast. I got peanut butter for you coming, I know how you love – I know how kids love it,' he corrected himself.

She looked at him, what was going on?

'So?' He was becoming impatient. 'And sit down,' he said, easing her into the chair next to Jay.

He stepped back and looked. 'No, over here beside mum,' he said, tugging at her to get up and easing her into the seat opposite.
'Mum.'
He was over-excited, hyper. She was beginning to feel uneasy.
'Right, what is it you want to eat?' he demanded.
She smiled wryly. 'Eh, toast, please, just toast and butter.'
'Oh,' he said, the disappointment seeping out as his smile faded to a look of distaste.
'Jay, looks like you're the only one for peanut butter today then. Maybe tomorrow?' he shot a glance at Lilly. She nodded, avoiding eye contact, it was too intense – he was too intense.
Breakfast reminded her of a pantomime where everyone plays their part. He played everyone's, even hers.

Dolls. She hates dolls. She hadn't seen one, not since then. She never wants to, never. She's no longer lying flat on the floor but screwed up in a ball, fists clenched so tightly her nails are cutting into her palms. She notices and likes it. She clenches tighter. Her feet are the same, toes squeezed tight into her foot. All her muscles ache. Her legs, her arms, all go slack on her release. She shrinks from it, from him, into herself, more gently this time. Here is better. Here was always going to be better. She wants to go where it's nice. She's closing her eyes. Somewhere without him, somewhere all hers. But it's not – her eyes flick open – not anymore. He's there, his footsteps in her mind, she kept him at bay for so long but this, all this let him in. She's clenching her fists, the trickle of blood running the length of her hand. Not now, not there, it's mine.

★

The sky seemed heavy, darker than it had before. He glanced up at it as he ambled home, not because he thought it would rain but because it was dominating. He felt threatened. He talked to himself angrily, tried to see a way out of his thoughts. He couldn't. There was no logical way out, no reasoning with his conscience. The grit of the road distracted him, the crunch of the stones beneath his shoes with each step acted as a deterrent to anything new creeping in – he focused on it. Crunch, heave, crunch, heave, crunch . . . then he saw it. It had been there. He'd felt it from the moment he'd broached the edge of the village but now it caught his eye. With each step he felt it move, the depth of its shadow more menacing than ever before. Little boys, they like to frighten themselves. He and his brothers would play games, pretend there was something to run from in the 'big bad woods'. That was its name, the game, he remembered. He remembered how they'd play until they believed it, until their fear was real.

It crept along the field as he quickened his pace, a sinister giant lurking in the distance. His breathing was becoming faster. He could feel the lunge of his chest as he ran, his hands clenched into fists, punching at the air as he charged toward home, constantly fighting to be free of her but she was there, always there looming beside him. He heard a yell. It distracted his thoughts. He would have wondered who it was if not for the dryness in his throat. He knew it was him, the noise ringing deep inside his ears. He hadn't known it but he had yelled out as he quickened his pace, half in fear and half as an outlet for the surge it took to get him away from there, to get him home. He was pushing himself more than ever before, more than when they played the Big Bad Woods, more than when he got sucked into his own illusions. This wasn't the same. It felt different. It wasn't a game he could run home from and shut the door. This was life and he was living it.

The door ricocheted off the wall as he came crashing through it, swinging off its handle into the hallway just to fall back into it as he slammed it shut. He saw it, its shadow as he slammed the door in its face. He saw it retreat, waiting. She was there, in its darkness. He could see her. He rubbed his hands over his face in exasperation as his head sank back against the door, he wanted to sink into it, be absorbed, vanish. It was wet, he realised, his face. He wiped the blur from his eyes and noticed he'd been crying. His nose was dripping too. He wiped it on the back of his hand just as his mother peered around the wall.

'Tommy?' she said, quite aware it was him but confused by his appearance. 'You okay? Did you get to the shop?'

He swallowed to clear the dryness from his throat and attempted to speak. He couldn't, his tongue caught in his mouth. He worked at the saliva before trying again. By now she was directly in front of him, her hands working frantically at the dish-cloth hanging from her apron. She looked at him. He was flustered, stressed, his school bag slung across his chest, two empty hands rubbing frantically at his face. The floor was bare; he'd brought nothing home. He was upset; she knew that by the tears in his eyes.

'Maybe you should sit down, rest, catch your breath?'

She didn't know what else to say. She didn't ask what was wrong because she didn't want to talk about it, didn't want it to be about his father. She wanted to keep believing they were as okay with him being gone as she was. She turned on her heel, not wait-ing for him to follow, and walked away, past the kitchen and down the hall. That old familiar hall, she thought, biting her lip to keep the tears at bay at least until she reached her room. That was all she had to do, make it out of sight. She wasn't ready, she knew it then. She couldn't cope, not with tears and upset. No, she would wait a little longer, just until things had settled down. She leant against her door and eased it shut, lifting the latch with her fingers so as to keep it silent while it closed. She was gone.

Suzie's head sank, she knew what it meant when Ma bit her lip, she knew it would be another while before they had her again. Tommy hadn't moved. She thought he would follow as advised but he'd stayed put. She would have to go to him.

'Tommy?'

It was the same tone as his mother – nervous inquisition. He was beginning to abhor it.

She looked at him, silent.

'I saw the church, that's all, I haven't really seen it since, not like I did today.'

He knew he had to lie. They would never understand.

'You've seen it plenty of times,' she smiled, easing an arm around his shoulder and guiding him toward the living room.

'Not like today. I'm going to my room,' he added, shrugging her off.

'Do you have the list? I'll pop back into town and get the things?'

His back was to her, he didn't bother turning around. 'No, I lost it,' he said solemnly.

'It's okay, I'm sure I can work it out,' she uttered, her voice quietening with the weight on her mind. She had thought it had been too easy, they had all come through things too unscathed.

His room was dingy as he entered. He had forgotten to pull the curtains when he got up. That pleased him now, it suited the moment. He had calmed by the time he closed the door and sat upon the bed. Too much upset did that to him, made him listless.

Temporarily anyway. He took a moment and breathed. Strange how we do that to settle ourselves, he thought, breathe and notice it. He did it for a moment or so before it all flooded back: the ladies in the shop, the wood, Mrs Christmas Eve, Lila, his father. He burst into tears, legs crossed beneath him, and rocked on the bed. What could he do? How would he ever explain? He jumped at a creak in the floor and turned toward the covered windows. He wondered if it was her shadow he could see twitching beyond them. His stomach was in his mouth, but he fought it, he jumped to his feet and drew back the curtains. Nothing. There was nothing and no one. He breathed a sigh of relief.

The box beneath his bed caught his eye. It wasn't new to him; he had spent a lot of time with it recently. He yanked it free from beneath the frame. It had originally been too large, so he had adjusted it by crushing down the sides, making it a little easier to squeeze in and out. It was less trouble with each new attempt; either he was getting better at it or the box was waning under the pressure. The smell was a special part of the process, one of the best bits, he thought, as the damp rose to meet his nose. It was thick and musty, reminded him of the old outhouse, damp and earthy. It was an old box he had gotten from Nik Naks shortly after his father had died, they didn't tend to have spares but under the circumstances they made sure to find one. He fingered it now, still slightly damp, but crisping up with each new day inside the warmth of the house. It was sun-bleached and dirty, old and loved, he reckoned, preferable to a new crisp one. It had lived beneath his bed for six weeks now. It should have been longer but it took him the first few weeks to get around to fetching it. He had been quick enough to ask, it just seemed to take a while to get as far as collecting it. All the same, it was here for keeps. There was no lid, just folded-over flaps, two of which were ripped and battered from continual use. He had considered cutting them off to save any hassle, for at that point he imagined they would be being sealed shut and propped above the wardrobe for good. That hadn't been the case. Instead, it stayed there for the first few days, then he took it down and hoaked through, this became a more frequent thing until it seemed pointless going through the rigmarole of hiking himself up on a chair to prop it up there. No, it got an upgrade to lying beneath his bed. A privilege, he thought, for an old worn box. A privilege doing what it was doing anyway. It had an important job: it held his father's clothes.

He unfolded the flaps and eased them out, raising them to his nose to smell the scent of alcohol; it was fading and mingling with the muskiness, nice all the same. First was the shirt. It was an old one he had found draped on the chair in the old playroom, probably still there from the night before he died but the one he was wearing at the time was too blood-soaked to be good for anything. It felt like him, big and soft. Then came the trousers. He was wearing these when they found him. They were no good for burying him in, too grubby, Suzie had thought, so they were returned by the funeral home later in exchange for a better, more respectable pair. A better pair would have meant nothing to Tommy. It was this pair he wanted, this pair that held all the feelings, all the emotion. Then the cool of the glass slipped into his hand and he truly felt like him. It was the bottle he'd had that day. Tommy had saved it from the bin when Stan got rid of it for being 'the curse of this family'. Tommy didn't see it that way, he knew better, he just saw it as him, Pa.

He stood now, twelve years old, five foot two, swamped in his father's old clothes. Trouser legs and shirt sleeves flailing, half the length again as his limbs but he liked it that way, it had to be that way. Rolling them up would defeat the purpose. He wanted to be with him, be like him, experience it; to make the things fit would be pointless. It was different today, as he adjusted himself in the baggy clothes, hiking them up at the waist to stop them falling off as he wandered back and forth in front of the window. It felt slightly wrong, sordid even, what he was doing, had been doing all this time. He looked down the length of himself and smiled as the saltiness rolled over his lip and into his mouth. No it wasn't, he was keeping him close, alive, that's what he had been doing all these weeks. He had found himself compelled to do it more often lately, when anything came into his mind, when the guilt crept in, he would close himself away in here and make his peace with it, but today was different, it wasn't working like that, like before. Instead he felt something lingering. It was just a feeling, he told himself, as he lifted the empty bottle to his mouth and pretended to take a swig, but it wasn't working, this pending feeling was getting stronger like a pressure inside his head just waiting to explode. He desperately needed fresh air. He tore at the clothes to get them off. It wasn't hard. On his release the trousers freed him and the shirt pulled over his head in one fearful tug. He looked at them now, lying strewn on the floor as though they were lived in, really lived in as his father would have done. He shook the thought free and thrust them back into the box before stuffing it beneath the bed. It was more of a rough shove than the usual tentative one he would have given before but he wanted them out of sight before he sped outside. He couldn't let them see; they would never understand.

The air was cold on his face, a harsh contrast to indoors. Perfect. He needed it, something to shake him free of the smog he felt smothering his every breath. It was with him inside, it went with him to school, he even felt it on his walk home but just then, for that moment, he could breathe freely. It didn't last. The weight of the wood banging at his side made him turn and stare. He saw it, like a blanket of darkness, lurking in the distance. They lived so near Thickets Wood it had been like a garden to him. Not now, not anymore.

He watched as Suzie walked toward him. She was on her way back from Nik Naks. She was so close to it, too close he thought, close enough for it to reach out and grab her. Fear filled him, a fear he couldn't comprehend, but he kept still, didn't flinch, didn't call out to her, just watched, waiting to see what would happen, his sister walking with the army of trees growing ever smaller behind her. He watched, waiting. For what? He didn't know, but he was waiting all the same.

'You going to help me with these bags or not?'

It was Suzie, he could hear her, see her mouth move, but it didn't seem like she was speaking, not to him anyway. It didn't seem like he was there.

'Tommy? God you really are a mess today,' she remarked, her shoulder banging his as she waded past through the open door.

'Where are Stan and Ethan, I haven't heard them?' he asked, noticing the silence for the first time.

'In the wood, playing,' she called, already indoors unloading the shopping.

'The wood,' he noted, trying not to impart any kind of fear.

There was a yell, this time not from him. It was one of his brothers. They were playing Big Bad Woods.

Ethan came charging up the field running parallel to their land, fought to gain distance too quickly and, tumbling onto the ground, he stared behind him, struggling onto all fours as he backed away. Tommy stood, frozen as he watched. Staggering to his feet, Ethan hurtled toward him, throwing himself over the fence, landing hard on his back before charging across the grass, yelling, 'Tommy!'

Tommy stared back, his body moving forward, although he didn't want to. 'What's wrong? Where's Stan?'

'We, we were playing . . .'

He paused, gasping for breath.

'You were playing Big Bad Woods and what?'

'He started talking about the lady of the wood, telling me all this stuff and I shit myself, that's what happened!' he choked, his hand against the wall of the house as he caught his breath.

'What lady, is the —'

'Boo!' cried Stan, jumping out from behind the far corner of the house. 'Had you going there,' he laughed, tears in his eyes as he tried to compose himself.

Tommy looked between the two. Ethan's colour was coming back, having realised it was all one big joke, and Stan thought himself the tough guy, having not got sucked in. But Tommy knew better. He had heard the talk in school, the silly stories kids were making up to scare one another, but he had heard much more than that. He had heard what was really going on and he wasn't laughing. He glanced back as Suzie ushered them all into the house under the pretence it was going to rain, watching as the shadow crept up the field. *She* was in it.

13.

She jumps. A noise. Not in here, but through there, beyond the changing wall. She recognises the sound, it means food. She scuttles toward the door and peeks in: a bowl, on the floor by the cot. Her stomach rumbles. She places her hand on it in the hope of silencing it but it does it again. She wonders why she bothers. It has never worked before. Hope, she thinks, there's always the hope. They do it more often now, drop in food. A grin creeps onto her lips. She wonders if it'll be porridge.

Clank.

That's the spoon.

She doesn't like metal in her mouth. Never will. She uses her hands. Metal is wrong in your mouth. Metal tastes bad. She's running her tongue around her teeth. They feel free from it but she remembers when they weren't. The taste. The taste of metal. She won't use a spoon. She's licking her teeth, her head shaking. She pulls the sheet over her head and walks toward the bowl. Hands, always hands.

The steam is rising from the dish as she slips her fingers in. It's hot and sticky. It doesn't matter, hands are better than metal, she thinks, blowing frantically to cool the dollop down before eating it. Better than metal. The skin on her fingers is red, it burns to touch.

After breakfast he led her back upstairs to brush her teeth. It was an old toothbrush, pink with a faded picture of a mermaid on it. It made her cringe to think it wasn't hers but he towered over her as she brushed; she wasn't about to complain.

'There's one last thing before you're ready,' he beamed. 'Did you notice Jay, downstairs, did you notice her brace?'

She hesitated in thought. She had no idea what he was talking about until he gestured toward his teeth, then it clicked, he meant the metal.

'Yes,' she said.

'Well I have a little thing here to put on your teeth to make them pretty.'

'But they are pretty,' she interrupted, her fingertip gliding over the surface of her upper set.

He looked displeased. 'I know, but they'll be even prettier with this,' he smiled, holding up a fine piece of metal.

She took a step back, 'I don't really want it to —'

'Trust me, it won't hurt one bit.'

'But —'

'There's no but, now come here and let's get this done,' he said, lunging for her arm and pulling her toward him.

'Please don't, please, please, please, please don't,' she begged, tears blurring her vision as she scrabbled at his hand to release her.

It was pointless.

'Unless you lie still, I'll end up gluing your mouth together. Your choice little one. Open up for Daddy or risk your lips sticking to your teeth.'

He had dropped the pleasantries, he meant business and he wanted no faffing around.

She heard every word and decided it wasn't worth the risk, she would do as she was told, just as she had done so far. It was pain-free, as he had said. He simply lay her down with an open mouth, resting his knees above her shoulders to keep her still, his weight bearing down on the towel beneath her head as he eased back her lip, making her teeth more accessible. His fingers tasted of a mix between salt and butter. It was a horrible taste against the fresh mint in her mouth, made her want to spit them out and rinse clean. She couldn't and she knew it, so she did the next best thing: she shut her eyes and thought of something nice. The glue had little scent as he squeezed a dollop onto each of the front six teeth, pressing the piece of wire down as he went along. She barely knew he was doing it. It felt like forever by the time he released her, having made her lie with her top lip hoisted up for an unbearable length of time while the glue dried. It was difficult to gauge how it felt at first; her mouth was too dry to move her lip, let alone talk. After a few sips of water from the tap she got to grips with the boulder in her mouth. It felt like he had laid a train track across her teeth, pushing her lip out to the door, but she knew that wasn't true, if only by feeling for it with her fingers.

He smiled, joyous. 'Perfect.'

She made an attempt at a false smile back but the ends of the wire chafed the inside of her cheeks and instead made her grimace.

'You'll get used to it. Now, let's find you something to wear, Julia,' he continued, a bounce in his step as he led the way to the bedroom.

Metal, she looks toward the spoon, shaking her head. No. No, not metal. She looks to her hand, sticky from porridge, and feels for the back of her dress. She grabs hold of the hem and wipes her fingers clean as best she can with the odd re-suck of a finger to help any drying bits lift. She doesn't like to be dirty, not if she can help it, not where she can see it anyway. It's nice to be in control. She looks to them and then feels for the sheet draped over her shoulders. Somewhere nice, she thinks. Not the wood – nice. Nice and safe.

★

She awoke, but not entirely. There was a continual thudding reverberating through her window, encouraging her to drowse in and out of sleep for a moment longer; it added a sort of lullaby rhythm to her now wakeful dreams. She tossed and turned, dragging the duvet on and off her head before resigning herself to getting up; it felt premature but she had little choice, she was awake.

Howard and his early starts, she thought, drawing back the curtain to see him wielding an axe. She had known he would be chopping wood today; she just hadn't betted on it being so early. An oversight on her part; she should have known better.

The sky was dim, mist hung heavy in the air. She could feel the chill passing through the glass. It was going to be a bitter day, she thought, a gentle shudder reverberating through her as she glimpsed the woods from the corner of her eye. She lingered there a moment, caught in the stories she had heard. No, it was nonsense. Absolutely no reason for her to waste her time thinking about it. Not really anyway, she reassured herself. Not now. After all, so much time had passed and she had made good with her past. Resting her forehead on the glass, she peered down at Howard. A slow smile crept on her face; he was a good man, great even and in that moment she was overwhelmingly thankful for him. Still rationalising the thoughts mulling around her mind she drew on the cardigan draped over the radiator from last night, and her cotton bottoms – Howard liked to joke about them, said they were like men's long johns. They're not, of course, they're just comfortable.

She wondered if he had eaten already as she made her way toward the kitchen, the cold of the floor seeping up through her bed socks. She assumed he had, given that the pile of wood stacked behind him was clearly a few hours' work; he would be incapable of that on an empty stomach.

'You eaten anything?' she called through a crack in the door, scared to open it any wider for fear of letting out what little heat there was. He didn't hear her at first with the whoosh of the axe, she had to repeat it; this time she timed it more appropriately. She stood twitching, irritated at having to linger in the cold.

'Yes, thanks Lou, up and made porridge earlier,' he said, wiping the sweat from his brow. 'Left you some in the pot.'

She smiled, it was just like him.

'You going to take a break with me while I eat it?'

She never was one to eat alone, he thought, smiling back at her just-visible face. 'Will do, could do with one. Just you let me know when you're ready.'

It took no time to reheat the pot and pour the tea. What took a little longer was struggling her way through the door with the tray. She knew he'd prefer to be outdoors, meant he could put his feet up and smoke; she'd be inside all day, it wouldn't kill her. That she doubted in the first ten minutes when the cold bit at her face. Needless to say, she survived.

'Pyjama day?' she grinned.

'Pyjama day,' he nodded, the cigarette smouldering a tone of red that made her feel warm inside.

Pyjama days were their little ritual, theirs and theirs alone. They were the days they spent all their time at home, going nowhere. Today was ideal for one. Howard would be outside at it all day and Lilly had nowhere to be and no one to see. She could potter, cook, read – it was perfect.

'Been splitting those logs nearly three hours already and I've hardly made a dent on it,' he sighed, pushing himself to his feet. 'Be enough here for the whole winter by the time I'm done.'

'Just don't be getting tired and sloppy,' Lilly said with a grimace, remembering when he sliced the edge off a finger. It was not something she wished to relive.

'I won't, don't you worry,' he said, lifting his hand and glancing over the scar.

'I'll be keeping an eye,' she muttered, more to herself than him, but he heard and smiled anyway. He loved how she cared.

The kitchen was her first port of call; she liked them to have something nice to eat with their coffee mid-morning so she set about baking a batch of cookies. What they would be largely depended on what was left in the store cupboard. She knew they had chocolate but what else would be a mystery until she finished the dishes and had a chance to look.

Chocolate. Hazelnuts. Flour. She knew she had the rest, and if the flour was short she could substitute with oats, she thought, catching a glimpse of the bag where Howard had put it back earlier, on the wrong shelf; it was a sign of his early start. That was settled then: chocolate and hazelnut cookies.

They were quick to make, five to ten minutes now that she had cookie-making down to a fine art. She had just popped them into the oven and was busy licking the spoon when there was a thud at the door. It startled her, making her jump. She hadn't expected visitors, she never did, not unannounced, but it bothered her very little. She was happy to be seen prancing around in her comfies. She cared little for what other people thought.

'Sorry if I pounded the door too loud there. Don't think you heard me the first time darling.'

It was Farmer Drey.

'Not at all, come in, it's freezing,' she said, ushering him toward the kitchen.

He was carrying a large grubby sack, the sort used to bag potatoes; she wondered what was in it.

He noticed her questioning expression and volunteered an explanation.

'Got the new pickings here. Said I'd drop them down when I got the chance. I know the old man's up to his eyes these days,' he smiled warmly.

He had a well-lived-in face, softened by laughter and toughened by hard times. His eyes were an aquamarine, his hair dappled with grey. He looked every bit Howard's match in age despite being ten or more years his junior. She wondered if she had a part to play in that, if she kept Howard young. The Dreys had no children, through choice or not she was never sure. She thought perhaps that added to his aged appearance. He had a large working farm with no inheritance, not of direct blood anyway, and no sons to ease the load as he got older. It couldn't be easy. She felt for him now, as though they could be lonely, just the two of them up there; he'd have made a great father. He did have family: he had them, she thought, contenting herself with the notion. He was like an uncle to her, not because they spent a lot of time together – they didn't – but because he was Howard's closest friend and she had known him all her life here.

'Smells good. What you got cooking?' he asked, sniffing the air.

'Cookies, might get one for the road if you're lucky,' she said. 'Just go on out,' she added, motioning toward the back door. 'I just have to wash these few things up.'

She watched through the window as they came together, settling themselves on the back steps to have a chat, the sack resting where Drey set it, by the post at the top of the steps.

'There she is,' Drey said with a sigh. 'Up ahead, blowing away bold as brass,' he continued, straining through the mist to see the woods.

That was something she had noticed about Drey. He personified everything, referring to it as 'she', but now, now he may have meant something.

'What do you mean?' asked Lilly, her hands still damp, having not dried them properly before coming out, something she was beginning to regret as the cold stuck to them like ice. She pulled them up into her sleeves and gripped the warmth of the cardigan around them; there was a slight improvement.

'Just that she's so alive on days like this.'

She followed his gaze and saw the woods for the first time that day. The trees stood like stick men, jagged and brittle, fighting their stance against the mist. They struggled, the breeze seemingly adding to their strain. She found herself pitying them.

'You been hearing all the talk?' he added, all three unflinching, mesmerised by the trees' battle.

'Aw, yes. Even young Lilly here's been asking about it,' Howard said wearily, his boots weighing his feet to the ground as he fought to straighten his legs and give himself a little more ease before getting back to cutting. His younger years of fluent mobility were gone and he knew himself well enough to know that a creak in a knee would do him no favours this afternoon. Even if he could handle it, Lilly would be quick to spot it and put an end to his day's chore.

'Well I don't know,' uttered Drey, loosening the scarf around his neck so as to breathe a little freer, 'I'm not one to be taken in by ghost stories and nonsense but there could be something in it.'

Howard spluttered, choking on his swallow. 'Are you serious?' He hadn't expected that from Drey.

'Some things people do there's just no forgiving,' Drey said, his eyes still fixed.

'A wood's a wood. No need to be making ghosts where there aren't any,' said Howard, irritated at having to acknowledge his doubt.

'God's in most things, but he's not in everything, Howard, you gotta remember that from time to time. You of all people should know it,' he said, glancing between them, reminding them that life wasn't always so good.

'I have a farm hand, a young boy. He got talking about his father's brothers and how they went out there years back, way before the stories started, and one of them never came back. Turned out he'd been having his fun blowing up rabbit holes with little homemade petrol bombs. Used to siphon it outta his dad's truck and run around at night, burning these poor wee things up. Well that was all okay until this one night when he threw one down a burrow beneath one of the big trees in Thickets Wood. Nothing happened to him then, no, not for a week or so. Then that day, with his brothers, well they lost him, he just vanished apparently. Later that night they found him, beneath a fallen tree. Thought it was some big accident at the time but once a few more things happened and then their dad told them he'd been having trouble with him arsoning rabbits, they put two and two together. He wasn't right apparently, couldn't have been to be hurting nature like that, but when you hear all these things together you wonder.'

Lilly stood, silent. She would never have thought it; the two most powerful men in her life were succumbing to it, to everything. She was suddenly fearful, she felt sick.

'When I saw her that time, in the wood, I felt something come over me that I've never felt since. Thank God.' Howard shook it off and flicked a cigarette from his pocket. 'Some things we just can't understand,' he said, looking to Lilly, a tilt in his head against the wind, as he lit the cigarette now hanging from the corner of his mouth. 'Best not to go meddling.'

'I'm with you there,' Drey shrugged.

'Cookies!' blurted Lilly, quick on her heel into the kitchen.

They were fine, perfectly cooked except for a couple toward the back that were going to be all crunch and no chew – she happened to prefer them that way.

'One for the road?' Drey was peering in the back door.

'Don't eat it all at once,' she grinned, wrapping it loosely in paper, 'it's still quite hot.'

'Mouth like asbestos,' he laughed. 'Thank you Lilly.' He raised it in the air as though it were some great treasure. She smiled; it felt nice to give him a little something from their lives.

There was a great thud outside before the back door swung open and in came Howard lumbering the dirty big potato sack. 'You fancy sorting through this little lot, see what we've got to keep us going the next while?'

'Sure you don't want me to leave it for you?' She knew how he loved to pick the vegetables by hand. In this case it would just be sorting them, but it was one of his relaxants.

'No, this time it's all yours. By the time I'm done with this wood there'll be nothing left in me. You can let me know.'

The sack was tied at the top with an old piece of cord, knotted so tightly Lilly had to saw through it with the kitchen knife just to get in. She felt rather bad but she would mend it with a nice new string before they returned it to him. No doubt he didn't expect it back but neither Howard nor Lilly liked to keep hold of things that weren't rightfully theirs.

Inside was stuffed to the brim with all kinds of treats. That was the thing about eating seasonally – they were always dying to get their hands on the changing veg. She had aubergine, squash, beetroot, broccoli, a couple of fennel bulbs and cauliflower. Fantastic. Her head was already running through the variety of recipes she had to choose from. He knew they grew their own potatoes, leeks, carrots and apples so he had the good sense to omit them. It was thoughtful; he could have forgotten.

Bingo. She knew what it was to be: aubergine, butternut squash and honey bake, with a nutty breadcrumb topping. She was licking her lips just thinking about it. She filed everything into its rightful home in the store cupboard and dashed out to tell Howard all the lovely things they had got. She paused, just as she broached the top of the steps, as their earlier conversation came flooding back. There it was, dark and dismal ahead of her – it was alive, moving with her heartbeat. The mist was still thick, thicker toward the wood, hanging off the branches like a wet web. She felt fear creep in. It was slow and tentative, gripping her in a way she could not explain, but it was there.

14.

Damn wood! She's frantically shaking her head, clumps of hair in her hands. I said no wood Lilly! No wood! She opens her eyes and looks at her palms, they feel sticky. Her hair feels sticky. Dirty. She feels dirty. The wood is inside her; he is inside her, inside the good place. She doesn't like it. It used to be good, it was nice. She used to be able to control it, to switch it off. Now she can't.

Her mouth is dry, her tongue is sticking to the roof as she struggles to swallow. There's water, always water now. It's in there. She gathers herself and thinks herself lucky to have a distraction from there, from him. She raises herself on tiptoe and teeters toward the toilet wall. There is the shelf with a jug and cup. The pourer is funny; she didn't like it at first. It has a plastic bit that clatters down when it's tipped. It's messy too. She doesn't like that much either. Messy isn't good. She's a good girl, good, clean and tidy. A drip spills, she jumps. Nothing happens. This time she tips the jug on purpose; makes it spill on purpose. Nothing.

The clothes were getting tighter. Either that or she was becoming less compliant and their size was beginning to irritate her. It had been eight days. She had been counting. She will eventually loose count but for now, for now counting is keeping her sane. She hasn't been outdoors since she came here and there are certain rooms that she's not allowed into: the living room is one and the other front

148

room, which she assumes is the study because that is where he answers the telephone. He takes no chances. There are locks on both doors, high up so that even he has to stand on tiptoe. As for outside, that door is also locked but she gets to look out and see the garden. It has a swing and a slide. They're rusting and the slide is broken at the bottom but she still longs to play on them. He won't let her. Why have them for her and then say no? She can't understand. He gives no explanation. 'Another day. Don't worry, there's plenty to keep you happy indoors for now,' he'd say.

There were plenty of things to play with in her room, but after eight days they were becoming a bit boring – same old, same old. She had decided to take the tea set and have a tea party. It was nice except for Mum, sitting on the edge of her teddy circle, watching. He had insisted she stay. Lilly/Julia had watched as he had struggled to bend her legs into a crossed position. He had worked with her, all the time comforting her as he yanked and cranked at the legs. She wasn't able to do it, Lilly could see that. She reached out for a Barbie and tried to cross its legs just to satisfy herself that she was right. She was, of course. In the end he settled for having her sit bent-kneed on the floor, it was there she was sitting now, watching. It was all a little boring at first, until he left and she seized the opportunity to make it a real tea party with water from the bathroom. It was only next door. She was in and out on tiptoe before he could have suspected a thing. That was until the teapot got knocked over in a commotion between Pink Bunny and Shaggy Dog. Those were their names; he had the hand-written name tags around their necks.

'Oh, don't worry, Mummy will get it —'

'Mummy will do no such thing!' he bellowed, grabbing the pigtail of hair and dragging her sideways toward the bathroom. 'Get the towel,' he ordered, not letting up on the tug. 'Who told you could use water?'

She looked up at him, the view of his nostrils was clear; she could see the little hairs.

'There is no water in this room, ever! You're bloody lucky to get her things you little —'

He stopped himself, his hand just grazing her cheek.

'Get down there and dry it,' he said, slow and clear, lowering himself as he spoke until his nose was touching hers, his breath hot in her face and pungent with coffee.

Rather than close the door as he left, he pushed it wide open so the handle was touching the wall adjacent to the hinges, then he went next door, into what she assumed was his room. He was never far, never out of earshot. He watched everything she did, especially how pleasant she was with Mummy and Jay. That was when he was most touchy; that was when he was most unpredictable.

'Told you I'd get it,' she whispered smiling. 'Sssh now, no need to be upset, Mummy will just tidy this up then we'll go back to sleep until another day.'

She could taste the salt in her mouth as she spoke to them, the tears and snot rolling into one on her lip before hitting her tongue. She kept talking to them as though nothing had happened. She didn't want him to think he had upset her. She didn't want him to know.

'It's okay. You're okay,' she hears.

Her neck cracks as she draws her head from its tilt. Her feet, she feels her feet – she's wet herself. Then she notices her hands. The jug is light, empty even. She looks to the floor and sees the puddle she is standing in; she hasn't wet herself, it's water. She's spilt all the water from the jug.

'Okay, let's just get you over here, just slowly, sitting here. That's it.'

She's sitting on the cot.

'I'll just leave that here for you, for later.'

She doesn't look but she knows what it will be, a towel. She won't use it. The heat will dry her feet before they have the spill cleared up and are out of the room. They know that too, she assumes.

Swing. Swinging will help them dry. She is swinging her feet. Her eyes are closed; she's looking for them, always looking for them. They are all she knows, they are more her than she is.

★

It had been almost a week since the incident in the shop; Tommy hadn't been coping. The following three days he cried off school sick. He wasn't of course, not initially anyway.

'There's no fever Tommy. Are you sure you couldn't just make it in?' said Suzie, lifting her hand from his forehead and double-checking her own. 'Nope, definitely normal.'

'I just feel really sick. My head's sore, I'm woozy.' He wasn't lying, he really did feel nauseous.

She looked at him with uncertainty.

'I think I'm going to be sick!'

He bolted to the bathroom and flung himself onto the cold stone floor, heaving into the toilet bowl. This satisfied her. Tommy really was sick.

He heaved but nothing came up, there wouldn't be much but bile, he thought, as the retching tugged on the muscles of his stomach; he hadn't eaten since yesterday lunch time.

'Back to bed with you,' she said, having lingered by the door waiting to hear the splash. There hadn't been one but she was thinking the same thing as he was – there would be little food to

151

bring up anyway. In a way it pleased her to think he was ill. She had been worrying since he'd come back from Nik Naks yesterday; he hadn't been the same. He was jumpy. Not himself in the slightest. He would be one of the rowdier of the boys, perhaps it was because he was the youngest mainly, but it was in him to be playful. Thinking on it now, he hadn't quite been the same since their father had died; he'd lost a little of his mischievousness, become more self-absorbed and cautious. It wasn't in him to be cautious, not before. He came up with Pig Slide. It's a game they would play in summer. They would use Pa's ladder, then hoist themselves up onto the roof, the aim being to sit in a row on the top tile and slide off, seeing who landed furthest from the house. Being a bungalow, it wasn't the biggest drop, but enough for Ethan to sprain his ankle last spring on a bad landing. She smiled; they were a good bunch of boys.

'I'll bring you some water,' she said, pulling the quilt around his shoulders and tucking it in.

He resembled him, she thought, their father. She could see him in the turn of his nose and the deep setting of his eyes. He was more like him than the others. Not quite so much as herself, but of the boys he was the closest match. It saddened her, looking at him as he lay, eyes closed. It saddened her to look at Tommy and think of Pa. How can they go from this in their youth, to that in middle age? What can go so wrong? she wondered. The pain was beginning to show on her face and she was glad his eyes were closed so as not to witness it. It was her pain, not his. He would have been closest to their father, she thought, as she peered down at him. He didn't mind the drinking, was too young to notice the change.

She stuffed the quilt tighter around his neck to keep out any draught. It was a draughty house and she could hear the wind getting up outside. She had tucked Rolf in more times than she knew. He'd be out cold in his chair or on the sofa and she'd wrap him in a blanket. She hadn't tucked anyone in since and it made her realise how she had liked it, caring for him like that, like she – mother – never could.

They had been broken so long Suzie could remember little else. They were her parents, it was her family and that was how it was, sniping and glaring. Silence when there shouldn't be and silence when there should. The only time things were really happy was when they were apart, alone with the children. Even during her bouts of bed rest, mother could be loving and caring toward them so long as Pa was nowhere to be seen or heard. She would make things better for them now, she thought, watching him stir, her legs beginning to ache from standing over him. She and Stan could fix things for the others, a little at least. She smiled, an apprehensive sort of smile.

He awoke a few hours later. The feeling of someone peering over him still lingered. He glanced around; needless to say there was no one there. The curtains were still drawn since yesterday. They would remain so; he didn't want to see out, didn't want anyone seeing in. That was really it and he knew it, he wanted to shut them out, the woods, keep her away, stop her from seeing him, getting at him. Mrs Christmas Eve. The name should bring happiness, he thought, not this, not fear. He didn't like thinking over it, her name, didn't like having it in there. He yanked the quilt up over his head and turned toward the door, his back to the window. Out of sight, out of mind. He thought of something else, something nice. He struggled. His head was a mass of Big Bad Woods and shadows. That had been one of his favourite pastimes, playing Big Bad Woods with the others. Now it was all that came to mind when he searched for something nice, but it was dark, there were shadows in the trees, all around. She was in his head and he couldn't get her out. She had changed things, everything.

'I know you said you feel sick but I thought you ought to try eating something.' It was Suzie. She had knocked the door but he hadn't heard it. She imagined it was because the quilt was over his head, she couldn't be more wrong. 'Made some chicken soup.'

He could smell it before he raised his head. It smelt surprisingly good, made his stomach rumble.

'Sit yourself up and I'll prop up your pillows.'

She was a good nursemaid, plumping the pillows up behind him before easing him back and setting the tray on his knee. She wasn't sure whether to leave him or watch him eat – she chose the latter. It had been too long and she wanted to be sure he was getting some sustenance. He looked at the bowl of soup and the roll and hesitated. He had thought he was hungry. Now he wasn't so sure.

'You need it,' she said encouragingly. 'Your body can't get better with nothing to run on.'

She was right. He lifted the spoon and got stuck in. It was pleasant, creamy and not too hot, it could do with salt but he wasn't about to tell her that. He was distracted. He smiled on the realisation and bang, it was gone. He was right back there, where he had been, fighting to keep her away. He set the spoon on the side plate and nudged at the tray for Suzie to lift it and let him lie down. She was pleased enough, he had eaten half of it. If he did as well at dinner time he'd have something to run on.

When he awoke it was dark. There was a sandwich beside the bed. Suzie had left it. He was sleeping a lot. Maybe he was sick, he thought, feeling himself all over. No, he was perfectly capable of jumping from the bed and racing in circles around the house if he wanted to. Problem was, he didn't. He knew she was right about eating; he didn't want to make himself worse. He reached for the sandwich. It was slightly crisp to the touch, just the very surface. It had been there a while he realised, biting into it. It was soft and the cheese and ham tasted good. He was on the second half when he thought about it, when it somehow made its way to the front of his mind and sat there like a giant boulder; the window was behind him. For the first time, he didn't like it, the thought of not being able to see if anything happened there, if the darkness flickered, if the curtain twitched. Why would it twitch, how could it? But if it did and he didn't see, if she came in and he was facing away from her . . . He couldn't bear it. He spun around from where he sat and stared at it. Nothing. He had expected as much, it was just the what-if. Then another thing occurred to him – the door. He now had his back to the door. This was unbearable. He felt it now, already, the weight of the door, looming behind him. He had noticed while he lifted his sandwich. It was now lying on the floor in front of him. He had dropped it and hadn't realised. He had noted that the door was ajar, not a lot but a smidge, a finger's breadth, enough to stop it making noise on entry. Suzie had left it open for just that reason, he knew that. It was logical, so she could check on him without disturbing his sleep. He ached where he sat, the churning of the food in his stomach forcing him to wretch. He had to move, just a little, just enough to have his back to the wall, both window and door visible in his peripheral vision. It scared him, the thought of what or who could already be in there with him. Standing behind him. Under the bed. God, he had never thought of that until now, this very second. He grabbed his already crossed legs and hauled them further from the edge of the bed, out of reach of anyone's grasp. He knew what it felt like to be grabbed and dragged under the bed, Stan had done it to him a few times over the years thinking it would be funny. It had been, then. His stomach heaved into his mouth again. He had to do it, he knew he had to. This was the least safe position, he was defenceless sitting here like this, open to every angle. No, he had to do it. He was swift, so much so that his leg got caught in the quilt in the turn as he threw himself against the back wall above his bed. It caught his knee and left his foot hanging exposed over the edge. He tore it free and pulled both knees close to his chest, his feet securely in front of him, out of harm's way.

The floor beyond the door creaked. His eyes darted for something to grab hold of, something big and strong.

'Oh, you're awake.' It was Suzie. Of course it was. He breathed a sigh of relief.

She looked at him curiously and rested her behind on the edge of the bed.

If she's sitting there, there can't be anything beneath it, he thought, his eyes drawn to look at the position of her feet tucked slightly beneath the frame. It must be okay.

'Tommy!'

He looked up.

'Did you hear me?' She was becoming irritated.

'No, sorry.'

'How are you feeling?' He didn't look well. He was pale, antsy.

'Much the same. I think I just need to keep sleeping,' he said, an attempt at a smile creeping into view. It didn't quite meet its full potential but she had seen a glimmer of it nonetheless. It was more than she'd seen all day.

'Well we'll just settle on you being home again tomorrow,' she smiled, tousling his hair as she stood up to leave.

'Would you close the door tightly this time?' he asked.

It wasn't a strange request, and she did it without question. Had she known why, she might have responded differently, but she was none the wiser. He was sick, he wanted peace to sleep for the night.

He wouldn't lie down again, not now that he had realised what he had. He had to come up with a way to sleep sitting here. He was willing to sleep. He thought that might clear things up in his head, change his perspective on them when he awoke. He just wouldn't lie down. Lying down obscured his view, he knew that through years of sleepless nights. It also made him vulnerable. The thought gave him goosebumps. Like a gentle breeze they blew over him from his feet upward, every hair follicle standing on end, all the way up to his scalp. He felt them making their way. It was a brief stay; they had gone by the time he realised they were in his hair. He quite liked them, they reminded him he could feel more than terror. It didn't take him long to fall asleep, fighting with your inner demons can do that sometimes, exhaust you past caring. He was there, he had fought past any point of wakefulness, he just wanted it to go away.

The creak awoke him. It was quick and sharp. He bolted upright, rigid. His breathing was quiet, shallow, as he waited for the door to open and Suzie to peer in. It didn't. She didn't. He heard it again. This time it lingered. He wasn't sure if it was in his head. He wouldn't know. The quiet that followed drew his attention to the humming in his ears. His brain was humming to him but there was more than that, there was a whistling, a low, distant whistle at the furthermost part. It coincided with the hum, complimented it. The hum he knew, it was just a head noise, it was what his father called 'the well'.

'You ever get stressed out Tom boy, just focus on the well. Works for me every time,' he'd say.

It's the noise the blood in your head makes; he's focused on it now. The whistling's still there, he can hear it, see his father doing it. It's not his father; he knows that. It's something else. He jumps to his feet, remembering that Suzie had stood there and knows he has no choice, he has to see.

His fingers clung to the knob, they twitched, he thought it felt warm and drew them back abruptly. He stared at it for a second, his hand clenched tight to his chest, before fingering it once again. This time it was cold. It had been all along; it was his mind playing tricks on him. There was a slight resistance before it clicked in release, making him jump. The door sprang back toward his foot, banging to a stop on his toe. His heart thudded in his ears as he reached out to draw it back. His fingers grazing the edge before he sharply changed his mind and diverted for the handle. The floor creaked beneath his foot as he stepped back with the jolt; he chose not to have his fingers exposed to the dark on the far side. How could he be sure what was there? How could he risk it and not be sure? He couldn't, not where he couldn't see. No, the knob, the knob was best. It was silent in the pull; only the floor and his heart could be heard, by him at least.

This could be it, he thought, his toe just broaching the cold slab floor of the hallway. His hands were trembling uncontrollably, he saw them before he felt them. They were stretched before him, groping in the dark as his eyes struggled to adjust to the small shaft of moonlight seeping in from beyond the kitchen door. He wondered if he were mad. Should he have stayed where he was and ignored it? Maybe that's how she worked, maybe it was all about making you interested, making you need to search for her, seek her out. Maybe that's how she got you.

15.

Tommy, Tommy, Tommy, Tommy, Tommy.

She's rocking cross-legged on the cot, sheet draped around her shoulders protecting her from the cold brought in by the noise in the ceiling. She has goosebumps. It does that to her, the noisy thing in the ceiling. Better than too hot; anything's better than too hot.

No, no, no Tommy, no.

She's bumping her head hard against the wall behind her. She can see it. See some of *her* in it, in the happenings, in the dark. It was never there before. Not really, not clearly. It wasn't meant to be, not like this. She doesn't like it; she continues to bump. Bang it out. Bang it out.

'It's a lot for her. Leave her for a moment.'

As time passed, her questions became fewer; there were things she had come to realise. She would never be allowed out, he didn't so much as open a window to let in fresh air – everything was locked. When he went to leave the house, he would take her by the hand and lead her to the storeroom opposite his bedroom, shutting her in there until he returned. It was small, with no windows, no more than a box with a door. He had no intention of removing the wire from her teeth or stopping lightening her hair, despite the redness of her scalp or the blisters inside her cheeks – he didn't care.

She was becoming a toy to him, much like his dolls, except this one had fluid motion and could talk. Becoming was perhaps wrong. She always had been, from the moment he pulled the bag from her head – before that even, when he planned her – but she hadn't known that then, then she was Lilly and he was the man supposed to look after her. She was coming to despise what she had to do for affection, affection she was now beginning to resent, but had to encourage. She had to be Julia. Lilly was gone. There could be no spontaneous outbursts or radical actions unless they were predictably Julia. She had a manual, a concise manual. That was her bedtime story. He read a chapter each night, reverting back to the beginning when the final page came. She really was a real-life doll, manual and user guide included.

It was late at night, well past bedtime when she heard the thud and peered out. He had tucked her in exactly three hours ago, seven o'clock. It was rather early but she didn't mind, it was always slightly earlier on a Friday. She knew what day it was by looking at the calendar. She kept track in her mind a lot of the time but if not, if she got lost, which would happen from time to time, she used it to give her some grounding. There was little else to differentiate her days bar the title for them. Friday was her favourite day of the week, she longed for it. Bed was easier than being with them, him and the dolls. She could relax, a little at least. There was no role playing, which was a relief. Sometimes she hoped he wouldn't come for her in the morning for fear of getting something wrong, forgetting something she had been told. He didn't like to repeat himself. He expected her to listen and learn. No mistakes.

She had been Julia for almost two and a half months – seventy-three days. She was still counting. It was Julia he wanted, not Lilly. It was Julia he was teaching her to be. She had learnt that through more than her bedtime reading, indirectly, through bad-tempered comments when she made a mistake or reacted wrongly to something. She knew for sure that night, that night she looked out. She should never have done it, shouldn't have left her bed but it woke her and she was interested, nosey even. She was living in a world of play, but this was real, this was unpredicted and she wanted to see it. Break out of her role and just be, just for that moment.

He was kneeling in a fallen position on the upper steps of the stairwell, Mother sprawled beneath him where he had dropped her. She had changed since bedtime, he had changed her. His hand on her thigh exposed the tops of her stockings, pushing up the bottom of her dress, which was new too. It was pretty, short and floral. She had heels on her feet and lipstick on her lips, a deep shade of pink, it matched the dress.

'Get back!' he slurred, attempting to stagger to his feet. He was drunk. He slipped again in trying to lift Mother up, and crashed to his knees on the upper landing, this time the bottle of wine spilling over onto her cleavage; he licked it off.

'You're a little interloper, that's all you are. Won't ever be my special wee girl. Not likely, not the way you're coming along.'

He had laid Mother down and by now his breath was hot on Lilly's face, the stench of alcohol and fish forcing her to squint, to hold her breath in an attempt to push down the gagging motion in her throat.

'I had high hopes for you,' he paused, swaying. 'I did, thought you could do it. Maybe?'

'I'll get back to bed.' She was nervous, having never seen him drunk before. He seemed volatile, emotional; it made her uneasy.

'You do that, me and your mummy got some business to take care of,' he sniggered, wrenching her up from the floor and carrying her toward his room.

She looked at Mother's ever-pleasant face as he lugged her away *and envied it. She was in the better of their predicaments, she was submissive by nature, Lilly wasn't.*

She is no longer banging her head but still, silent. Her eyes blank as she stares into the distance. It's a moment of realisation. She sees it, for the first time she sees why.

★

'Tommy!'

Her shrill cry tore through the house.

He curled into himself, wrapping the quilt around his head, his hands pressing hard against his ears in the hope of blocking everything out. He wasn't sure which scared him more, Suzie or the dogs furiously trying to out-bark one another. Ordinarily, neither would have bothered him. Well, perhaps Suzie – her tone was a mixture of panic and impatience. This would usually mean she had caught on to something he thought he had got away with but today, recently, he knew that couldn't be the case – he hadn't left his room for over a week. As for the dogs, the fear of why they were so manic made the headache come back, closely followed by the sick. He wouldn't have cared before, would have thought it was nothing more than a caller or some rabbit they were vying for but lately, since he knew of *her* and the woods – it didn't bear thinking about.

They could see things, dogs, he was sure of it. Not just because they're quick but there's a part of them that reaches out to something greater than us. Pa had taught him that. He wouldn't forget because it excited him, the prospect of more than 'us', the you and I; it had excited Rolf too. He said he had seen it in them, not often by any means, but occasionally.

'The eyes will flicker, like they're watching something in the air, just before them but beyond you. One place you'll always see it is along the edge of the wood yonder. Don't like it much there, especially Beggar. Watch, you'll see my boy, gotta know them though, gotta know how they are,' he'd said.

He'd watched like a hawk for weeks, his father alongside when he could to point it out, but he never did see it, not for sure. The odd wee twitch he thought could be it but he wasn't close enough to them, wasn't quick enough to catch it fully. He hadn't heard the stories of Thickets Wood back then or it may have put him off the place, seeing that the pack wouldn't stray into it, not one of them. They would charge along its edge, a good yard or so away but they'd never venture in, even when he and the boys were playing Big Bad Woods alongside them. No, they had more sense, he thought now, his ears beginning to ache from the pressure of his hands. He eased them off a little.

'Tommy!'

The bedroom door sprang open, its force sending it pounding against the wall as she strode in close behind. He lay, still and silent, his breathing controlled in the hope she wouldn't see him, wouldn't think to look beneath the bed. He had been there since early yesterday evening. It had become too much sitting exposed to the room. He wasn't sleeping, couldn't breathe for fear of missing something moving, flickering even. Here he was almost invisible, nothing more than an old blanket stuffed beneath the bed, or so he hoped.

'Tommy.' The tone in her voice had changed from panic to relief as he felt a hand grip his shoulder. So much for being an old blanket.

'What are you doing under there?' she queried, tugging him out from beneath the bed.

He didn't answer, he just lay below the quilt hoping she'd give up and leave. No such luck – she whipped it back and stood above him glaring. With his ears free of his hands he could hear it clearly for the first time – the howling and yelping.

'I've wasted five bloody minutes running around this house looking for you, you idiot!' she yelled, a tight grip on his arm, pulling him to his feet. He was a sorry sight, pale and insipid looking, dark rings around his eyes from lack of sleep and lips, cracked and flaky from manic licking. It was his form of a comforter. He had done it since he was a little boy, licking his lips if he was in trouble, also a sure giveaway when he was lying. Pity fell on her face but it was brief, quickly overwritten by fear as the sound fell heavy on her ears.

'They're fighting for top dog Tommy, you . . . you have to get in there and sort it out.' She was beginning to choke, tears filling her eyes.

He looked at her blankly and for the first time in years saw her youth. There was as little as four years between them but it felt like a generation. She was mother, he was son, he and Ethan at least, but for that split second, she was his sister.

'Tommy!' she shouted giving him a jolt. 'You have to get out there, they won't listen to me. The others are at school. Anyway, they're no good either. You spent the most time with Pa and them, it has to be you.' She sighed, exasperated.

'But Pa . . . Pa was the leader not me. I just stood there.'

'It doesn't matter, he's gone and they're looking for a new one, they're fighting it out between them and I can't stop it. Hurry up or it'll be too late. Duster's too old for all this and he's not going to give in, not in this lifetime!'

He watched as she wilted before him, her shoulders limp, head low. She was lost.

The yelping grew louder, more intense as she held his hand and dragged him through the house toward the front door. He could hear it, could hear little else but that didn't stop him freezing once his foot broached the front step. He couldn't do it, he just couldn't. A wave of guilt surged through him, not just for the things before but now, for his dead father's memory. He couldn't let that down, not when so much of the sorrow in his life had been down to him. He couldn't fail at this as well. The air was cold in his chest as he inhaled and dived outdoors. It was worse than he expected, everything was.

'Enough, that's enough!' he said in the strongest voice he could muster, one hand opening the fence, the other gripping the wooden stick Suzie had been using.

'Back, get back!'

The gnashing of teeth scared him but it quickly ceased as he entered. Suzie stood awestruck, as did Tommy; they listened to him, they really listened to him. He felt more like his father in that moment than in any other he had tried to reconstruct or resurrect; his clothes or relived memories, this was what it was like to be him, this was what it felt like to be a man, head of the pack.

There was blood splattered on the dirt, he could see it glisten as he strode toward Duster. He was the oldest male, ten, maybe closer to eleven, long wavy black fur, pricked ears and a sharp nose; he was a beauty. The baying quietened as Tommy neared him, three feet wavering with his weight, the fourth close to his chest, protected. Tommy had no fear of the others, they backed away as he approached, they knew their place. Even Riley cowered, more submissive than the rest. He was top dog now, Tommy, to him they were all subordinates. He surveyed Riley on his approach to lift Duster out of there. He appeared fine, a few grazes but nothing serious. Riley would make a good leader when his time came; he was the next in line, Pa had told him that a year or so ago, but not just yet, Duster wasn't quite ready to give up his ranking.

Duster was heavier than Tommy thought as he struggled into the house and laid him on the cold stone floor, the yelping and whining subsiding once he was settled.

'You need to get me self-heal and chickweed, plenty of it,' said Suzie. 'Oh and yarrow. You know what it's like, the feathery one?' She was busy placing a cloth beneath Duster's head and upper body; there were no wounds further down.

'Tommy!'

She placed a pot of water on to boil as she waited for his response. He didn't respond, he just stood there, vacant. The moment had passed, the adrenaline was gone.

'Tommy, you get out there and help me save this dog or so help me, I'll never forgive you.'

His blinking became more rapid, he had heard her. He couldn't have another death on his hands, nor could he have any person other than himself looking at him with the abhorrence he saw flare in her eyes. It was more than he could bear, Suzie hating him, even more than being taken by *her*.

The wind blew up and the rain began to fall as Tommy stepped out with the basket in search of the plants.

'A coat,' he heard her call. He shrugged, he didn't mind a little rain, he minded even less when he realised that he was already standing in it.

The door closed with a clank behind him. His safety was shut up in there and he was out here. The goosebumps crept over him like seeping damp, he shivered. The trickles of red caught his eye, running in little streams along the gritted dirt and into wells on the edge of the path. He chose not to look at his arms, he knew now they were sodden in Duster's blood; he could feel it, the material stuck to his skin. He hadn't noticed before, hadn't thought to look. It was a distracting thought but the weight of the wood brought him back to the here and now. It loomed in the distance, banging like a great big giant on his head, the thud of his headache mingling with the throbbing blackness in the distance. Together they walked hand in hand with him on his search; he stepped, they banged, thudding along. He focused on that for a moment, hoping it might save him from what he knew was coming, what he felt in the pit of his stomach, *her*. It worked its way around him like a net. He was struggling to breathe, pulling at the neck of his T-shirt to loosen its grip. It wasn't gripping – he knew that – but it must be chafing him, choking him. Something was. He tugged at it until it eventually tore. He didn't care, it felt better, freer.

It didn't take long to find yarrow or chickweed, they flourished in the meadow grass, but self-heal was more of a problem and it was the most important, if he remembered correctly. It would help stop the bleeding. The rain ran in rivers down his forehead and into his eyes. They became blurred. He couldn't see; goddamn it he couldn't see a thing! The basket fell to the ground as he dropped to his knees, fists frantically rubbing at his eyes. He blinked harder still in the hope of washing the blur away; it was no use. The dull hiss of the rain hitting the grass began to echo in his ears, mimicking the bang of the throbbing. He could make out shadows, shadows of the woods. They were in the distance, not terribly far but far enough to put him at ease a little. Then something or someone moved, a shadow flickered between the trees as though it were nearing him. He blinked frantically, pushing himself to his feet. It was pointless, he still couldn't see but there it was again, jumping between the trunks. This time he knew for sure, there was no room for doubt. He reached blindly, batting out to feel for the basket; he couldn't come this far and return empty-handed. He chose to search with one hand and continue rubbing at his eyes with the other. This time when he opened them it was nearer, black as black in the smear around it. It was *her*, he was sure of it. As he turned to run something caught his foot, plunging him into the grass. It was long and wet, its edges slicing at his face as he fumbled, feeling for the basket and scavenging to gather what may have fallen out and put it back in before struggling to his feet and charging through the field back toward the house. He ran and didn't look back; his breath catching in his throat, the rain plummeting into his open mouth. He forgot about the self-heal, he just kept running. He dropped the basket in the doorway of the kitchen and didn't say a word. He was walking away, tears streaming from the sting in his eyes as Suzie lifted what he had gathered and dropped them into the pot to stew. She called after him but he didn't hear. The thudding was too loud.

What little comfort had been in his room before now was gone. He hadn't expected any, it hadn't crossed his mind, but he noticed the lack of it and sank onto the bed, hopeless. There was a click, a loud, demanding click in his head. It took hold of him, he jumped to his feet and drew open the curtains, opening the window – he was changing his strategy. Dim light surged across the room, illuminating the inanimate things that had become his allies and made them appear hopeful; he grinned. Turning back toward the window he was startled; struggling to keep his footing he tore back to escape across the bed to the far side of the room but instead tripped on his backward steps and fell, half over the frame and half onto the floor. He couldn't keep up with his thoughts as he tried to process what he had just seen. Had it been there before, had someone put it there while the curtains were closed? No, it was empty before, it had been, he was sure of it. He thought harder, clinging to the mattress and dragging himself over the bed only to scuttle across to the far wall adjacent to the door and stare. He blinked, he blinked again, this time rising to his feet and slowly walking back toward the open window. The sill was empty. It hadn't been a second ago. His fingers rummaged through his hair, he had seen them, weeds, weeds he'd been picking, they were there. Surely they fell off. He dared himself to peer outside the window and check but he couldn't; he had to, he had to know. His fingers pushed at the glass, a quick shove to open it far enough to get his head out. He didn't want to put his head out, not really but he had to know, he had to be sure. He looked out, peering at the ground before slamming the window shut and lunging onto the surface of the bed. He had been right, he had known it all along – there was nothing there.

It was dark when he opened his eyes. He had been sleeping. He twitched his feet, they were hot, he was hot. The damp clothes now stuck to him were warm with a mixture of rain and sweat. He did that a lot recently, sweated if ever he managed to sleep. He put it down to bad dreams. Something green caught his eye; he jumped as he noticed the chickweed strewn across his feet. He looked back and it was gone. He bolted upright, tugging at the now dry hair tousled around his forehead. He tugged again. It was real, it felt real, it felt more real with every pull. He was here, he knew with every jolt to his scalp. His bed was here, he hoped, otherwise what was he sitting on? God, what was happening? He reached for the sheet, his palm skimming the cotton. Yes, it was here. He hadn't meant for all this, he hadn't meant for any of it.

All he had wanted was to settle her, put her over to sleep, like they did, like they always did. He had just wanted to keep them from waking.

He hated that he was what he was, hated how he tainted everything. He was everything she wanted, Mrs Christmas Eve. He thought her name, this time with less fear. He was accepting it, accepting *her*. He was what they were talking about: the one who should worry. He was exactly that, the next in line. She was coming fast they said – *her*, Mrs Christmas Eve. Yes, he thought, glancing around the room, everything was here. Everything was real, but so was something else. He could feel it in the shadows. It was *her*, she was here. He had brought her to him. Today he'd done it. He had let her in.

16.

Her thick, lank hair wrapped around her fingers; the pain in her scalp, screeching out at her to stop, draws her back. She hasn't done that for some time, thought the habit had passed. It would appear not, she thinks, noticing the loose strands of hair on the floor. She's shaking. The quiver in her hands is only realised once she releases the hair and frees them to fall into her lap. She watches them for a moment, amused. There's a beauty to trembling in fear. She wouldn't have thought that so long ago, wouldn't have had the clarity to. She thinks to Tommy and sees him quivering, sees the fear. She's in there with them now; *he's* in there even more. The two of them together, tainted. It hadn't been that way before, before all this, before he was brought back, or forward more like. She had him away, buried. He was gone. He was nothing. Now he's there, here and there, living in everything, well, almost. She knows why, she heard when they said it. She listened and did it, didn't she? There's no good coming from it yet though – she's rocking – not seeing the good yet. Soon, maybe soon.

'Go on, just another bite,' he was smiling but she could see it was beginning to wane.

She hated white sauce. This was cauliflower in white sauce, even worse, and it was from a packet. She took a little on the tip of her fork and swallowed it down, attempting not to taste it. It worked, but the knowledge of what it looked like made her gag nonetheless.

'*It's one of your favourites,' he said, this time with a wrought-iron smile and clenched teeth, 'you know this.' The constant reminder of her bedtime story. She slumped back in her chair and sighed, it was draining pretending all the time.*

'*Julia,' he encouraged.*

He wasn't letting up, she could see that but she didn't like it, Julia or not, she didn't like it!

'*You'll eat this, you hear me? You'll eat this!' His voice was thunderous, his chair crashing to the ground with the force of his thrust from the table. He didn't stop to pick it up, simply stepped over it, scooped a huge mouthful onto his fork and rammed it into her mouth. He didn't stop, didn't let her swallow. Instead he squeezed the sides of her jaw, forcing her mouth open and continued ramming food down into her throat until it was stuffed. Tears blurred her eyes as she struggled to focus on breathing through her nose. The crown of her head pressed hard into the back of the chair, the only thing stopping him from breaking her neck with his force. He noticed the cauliflower on his hand and used her napkin to wipe it clean before fixing his chair and settling back down to finish his dinner. She didn't know what to do. She struggled to swallow but there was just too much food in her mouth to do anything. She struggled to spit it out but he had crammed her mouth too full even for that. Instead, she had to scoop it out with her hand, cutting through the chunks of cauliflower and dropping them back down onto her plate. She sat, terrified of what he would do, but he didn't flinch.*

'*Lovely dinner I think, might have that again next week,' he said instead, wiping around his mouth with the pink napkin before reaching forward to clear her plate onto his. She sat, still and* dumbstruck. What was she to do? Nothing, that's what. What would Julia do? She'd help. She slowly pushed herself free from the table and began to clear away the salt and pepper. It was a few more days before she saw another outburst.

'Julia, where is the cream for your rashes?'

She didn't have rashes so she didn't need cream.

'Julia?'

'I don't know, but they're away now sure, it must have worked, they're all gone,' she said, standing up and pulling at the sleeves of her T-shirt to reveal her inner elbows. 'See?'

He didn't look pleased. 'Don't mess with me, your rashes won't just go away, you've had them for years. Now where is the cream?'

In truth, she hadn't had it so she couldn't say no matter how hard he pushed her. 'I'm going to count to three. One . . . two . . . three,' and with that his hand flailed across her face. She grabbed her cheek and dashed past him, up the stairs and into her room. She didn't cry, she wouldn't let him see her cry – but he did. He followed close behind, sobbing as he slumped onto the floor beside her bed, scrabbling at her to turn around and let him hug her.

'I'm sorry,' he sobbed. 'I didn't mean to, it's just so hard sometimes. Please, I'm so sorry.'

She pitied him at moments like this, pitied his desperation to have her back.

'I'm not her, I never will be, you must know that. Just give me away, find someone else who can be, please. Or go back, go back to just Mummy and Jay?'

He stiffened up and looked at her. Tears ceased to fall from his eyes, his face frozen in animosity. She, his Julia would just leave him like that. Julia could never say or do that. He left and for the first time pulled the bolt on the top of the door. He left her there for two days. It was her first taste of how it was to be; she just didn't know it yet.

Her eyes squeezed shut; she sits tight to the wall, banging at it with her fist. Away, away – go away!

She sees it, the difference in him. It's getting too close, too close to the man he'll become, she can't look.

Away, away – she continues pummelling the wall. It's her vent, it takes her fear and transforms it.

Nice, go somewhere nice. Not with him. Take him away.

The battle to distance herself from him is getting harder. He's harder to shake. She can see him clinging on inside her head, a foot in the door wedging it open.

Nice. Lilly, that's it . . .

★

It was bleak outside. She was becoming accustomed to it. After all, it was late October and autumn was upon them.

'See you back here around lunch?'

Howard was loading up the truck and heading into the village to finish up a job before helping her out for the afternoon.

'Yep, lunch sounds great, you making it?' he grinned, old charmer that he was.

She smiled and turned on her heel. He knew she was; she had been preparing the soup since breakfast.

Their doors closed simultaneously, that of the truck ringing louder than that of the house. She waved through the glass, watching as he drove off. It was a rusty, creaky old thing, bouncing and rattling as he motored down the lane; she didn't like it much.

The soup was bubbling viciously when she entered the kitchen; she would wait until it was cooked through before she headed into Thatchbury for their afternoon buns. She could of course have asked Howard to bring a couple back, but she was looking forward to the cycle and anyway, with Sticky Fingers still closed it meant going to Rabbit's Burrow. The choice there was much smaller and she was fussy when it came to cream buns.

She had ten minutes or so before it would be cooked, she thought, pulling the fork free from the carrot and prodding the potato, maybe fifteen. Fifteen was better, gave her just enough time for a quick shower; she hesitated, that would be pointless, she was going to spend the whole afternoon lugging furniture around her room, she'd be a dirty, sweaty mess by the end of the day. No, she would preserve any warm water for later. This meant she could take her time getting dressed, a true indulgence; she tended to leave dressing until the very last moment rather than prioritise it, it made for a nice change. She sauntered up the stairs, her cardigan falling open as she enjoyed the last of the morning's heat. It was becoming less and less as the days were getting colder. It was only 9.15 and already she could feel the cold creeping in. This was partly due to the gap beneath the front door. She bent down from where she stood halfway up the stairs and glimpsed the outside peeking in at her. She had told Howard it was their main heat loss in winter but he disagreed.

'Little old house like this has leaks and gaps all over, an extra one beneath the door isn't going to go making much of a difference,' he'd said.

She thought different: any they could fix they ought to, before the cold really set in. Just then she had a thought. She would buy some material when she was in the village and make a draught excluder. He couldn't complain about that.

She was ready and dressed in five minutes; the clothes cool as she pulled them on. There was something nice about wrapping up warm. Half the joy of winter was pulling on big woolly jumpers, she thought. It made the changes in the seasons all the more enjoyable.

It was dry when she rolled her bicycle outdoors. The air was heavy and damp but at least it wasn't raining. She wondered if she were silly not to bring a coat but thought the better of it and started out without one. The sky looked clear enough and she already had her bum planted on the seat. She had made a start down her usual route into Thatchbury before it occurred to her – she had been so distracted in thought that she hadn't taken the long way, the one she had been using for nearly three weeks now. She pulled on the brakes, easing herself to a stop and thought hard about what to do. She felt so silly even considering it. She had been using the fire road for years, so she naturally headed for it unless she consciously flagged up 'do not go the usual route' before leaving.

The usual route led through Thickets Wood. She had been battling with herself for weeks now over this silly tale, this myth even, about Mrs Christmas Eve. Thing is, part of her knew it wasn't just silly, that deep-rooted part of herself that she kept hushing up. But it didn't hush, not like she wanted it to. There was still this low sibilant whisper. She could hear it when she was alone. When she closed her eyes. It was there hissing in her ear, begging her to listen, to let it in. Nudging her to doubt herself. Even now, standing here, she could hear it scratching to get in. But what had she ever done? Really done. Nothing. Nothing but be young and naive. She had no dreaded secrets she could think of that should make her fear anything, but all the same, it seemed juvenile not to listen to some of it, some things were just too much of a coincidence to overlook. She peered ahead at the woods just visible over the top of the hill and remembered the last time she chose to cut through them; her vision was becoming strained, she couldn't make out the moths or midges from where she stood. It would be of no advantage to push on, what would she gain? She turned the handlebars and cycled back the distance she had come, this time continuing on past the house and following the main lane into the village.

Rabbit's Burrow was heaving. She was later than intended after her little diversion so she was thrust into the throng of morning coffee-goers, something she had hoped to avoid. She spent her time in the queue eyeing up the selection of buns and tray bakes, choosing, then doubting her decision and choosing again. She managed to pass five minutes this way, a luxury she would not have had had it been a little quieter, and one she was not thankful for. Too many choices make her dither.

'Lilly! Lilly dear!' called Margaret.

Lilly gazed around the room, taking in each table and who was at it in an attempt to search out the voice.

'Lilly dearest, over here!'

She spotted the portly arm swaying above Margaret's head to draw her attention. She was at a table that sat smack in the centre of the room. It wouldn't be like her to care what others thought of her bellowing out above the noise, nor would it be like her to bustle her way through the crowd just to speak to her. No, she took the easiest, laziest option – she called above the noise.

'Lilly, get a cup of tea and come join us,' she called.

Lilly felt rather embarrassed having to shout over the crowd. 'Oh Margaret, thank you but I'm just in for a couple of buns then back off home . . .'

'Don't be so silly girl, get yourself something and join us for a little chat.'

Lilly sensed her enthusiasm and nodded in the direction of

the table she shared with Mertle. It would be a gossipy chat; she knew that much as she ordered two cream buns to go and a mug of hot chocolate.

'Do you mind if I take this?' Margaret asked the lone lady sitting at the table closest to theirs, already wrestling to turn the chair in a tight circle before the woman had a chance to answer. Thankfully, she agreed. Lilly smiled as she surveyed the situation on her approach. It was just Margaret's style, she was enthusiastic and pushy in everything she did.

'Lovely to see you this morning Miss Lilly, didn't expect to be bumping into you today. Just passed Howard finishing up at the pharmacy. About time Mr Haslow got that counter replaced, it was practically being held up by boxes.'

Lilly smiled. Percy Haslow had been waiting six months to have his new counter fitted; he hadn't realised Howard would have to dry out and season the wood before he could work with it. He had thought he would have it ready to go in a week.

'Yes, last day of the job today,' she grinned.

'I've been thinking of getting a new counter in the kitchen now you come to mention it,' chirped Mertle. 'Think mine's starting to look a little aged.'

'Oh there's Suzie Tinkit,' said Margaret, peering over Lilly's shoulder. 'The church had me deliver a —'

'They didn't have you,' interrupted Mertle. 'You volunteered.'

'Yes, my apologies, I volunteered to deliver a hamper the church had prepared for the Tinkits just the other day.'

'That was nice,' smiled Lilly, glancing around to see Suzie leaning, worn and somewhat bedraggled, against the counter.

'I thought so too. Nice to do a whip around when people are struggling, show what a community can really do,' said Mertle cheerily.

'Poor wee thing that girl. Whole family of boys to look after, one laid up and the mother no better. She thought maybe the mother was coming around a bit but no doubt seeing her in here means she isn't,' Margaret added, appearing rather glum.

'Which of the boys is laid up?' asked Mertle, quickly answering for herself before Margaret had the chance. 'Oh, I know. Young Tommy, isn't it? Been off school for weeks now apparently, teacher's starting to think he needs to send work home so he doesn't fall behind.'

Lilly sat quietly supping her chocolate, listening to the conversation like a bystander. She liked it this way.

'Remember not so long ago we were in Sparkle and Spools and he just raced out, bit strange-like?' Margaret directed the question at Lilly, not really asking, more stating a point. Lilly knew this and neglected to answer. 'Well according to Miss Suzie, he's been ever so strange. He's sick, no doubt of that, she says, but she's starting to think it's in his mind now too, much like the mother. Poor love, having two of them to care for. He hasn't left his room in weeks. No idea why. All something to do with the passing of their father I'd say, wouldn't you? No idea how these things are going to affect you until they happen, especially the young'ens. Terribly hard on them wouldn't you think?'

'That's dreadful,' Lilly sighed, recalling the funeral. 'He's only about twelve.'

'Well, needless to say, she appreciated the hamper. Keep them going in bits and bobs for a while. Other boys are great though. Bit worried about their brother, but dealing with the other things well. You know, their father and what else.'

Things fell quiet for a moment, all three wondering how it would be for Suzie, being so grown-up so young.

'I heard about the cake Mrs Rose baked for the Thompson

birthday party the other day. Did you hear?' asked Mertle. 'Three tiers high and every layer a different flavour. Apparently Mrs Pepperfield asked her to do some baking for in here. I can't wait to taste it. Does home orders now too, makes it and delivers it to the house.'

Margaret licked her lips. 'I'm looking forward to that. Might try baking one myself, give it to that poor family.' She watched Suzie leave.

'Sometimes people don't like too much kindness when they're struggling, just prefer to be left alone.' Lilly could see the surprise on Margaret's face. She had thought her comment wouldn't go down too well. 'I just know what it can be like, if you're struggling.' She was referring back to when she first came to Thatchbury. 'I know you mean well but maybe she'd rather deal with things in her own time, in her own way, without having to worry about someone arriving unexpected.'

'Or unwanted,' chirped Mertle.

Margaret was astonished, such a thought had never occurred to her, that kindness could be a nuisance, but she thought on it for a second and saw their point. 'Perhaps you're right Lilly, maybe space is the best healer, better than chocolate cake?'

'Yes, better than chocolate cake, this time I think at least. She didn't really look like a girl who wanted to chat, don't you agree?'

'She did pass without a hello, so yes, my hands are up, I surrender.'

They all shared a giggle at Margaret's expense before Lilly took heed of the darkening skies and jumped to her feet.

'Time I was off before the rain starts. Thank you for that nice surprise chat.' She smiled, lifting her bag of buns and winding her way through the array of tables and chairs standing between her and the door.

The clouds opened as she threw her leg over the bicycle and pushed herself into the road. She could see Howard's truck up ahead, strewn at an angle outside the pharmacy, cab door lying open. He wasn't inside, she could see that, but he must be thinking he will be else he'd have shut the door. Sure enough he dashed into the truck and slammed the door just as she reached him.

'You going home?' he called, leaning across and rolling down the passenger window.

'Have one last thing to get in Sparkle and Spools but other than that, yes,' she was spluttering a bit with the rain water.

He was already out and dashing around the nose of the truck to heave the bicycle into the back as she stepped off and ran up the lane toward the shop.

'I'll get you outside,' he called after her. She couldn't hear but had assumed as much.

She wasn't too picky about the material she chose for the draught excluder; after all it was for a purpose, not appearance. She chose a thick purple weave and bought a little gold ribbon for the ends. A bit fancy maybe but it would help add to its appeal when introducing it to Howard. She wasn't sure how to get away with not telling him what it was for before it was ready. Could always say it was for this nice new bedroom they were about to prepare, then discreetly move it to its rightful home. He was waiting outside when she dashed from the shop to the truck, one arm raised above her head in a silly, pointless attempt to keep herself dry.

'Home, Lou?' he asked, reaching across her lap to close her door.

'Home it is,' she grinned; she so loved his little ways.

The truck rumbled along the dirt roads as they made their journey home, much of the way directly alongside Thickets

Wood. She found herself pleased to be in the truck and not out there, not at such close proximity. Even in here, the passenger seat was beginning to feel a little uncomfortable. She watched as the trees darted past, one, then another, thick and fast.

'Don't be doing that, looking out like that. You'll go making yourself sick.'

She jumped.

'You okay?' he queried. 'Looking a bit lost there.'

His face was soft, the creases in his skin gentle like folds in cotton.

'I'm great, in a daze that's all.' It was a lie and she hated herself for telling it.

'So long as you're sure,' he added inquisitively.

She looked at him for a moment, not at all surprised at the doubt in his voice. He knew her better than she knew herself at times.

'Do you think what I did was so wrong?'

He turned to her in surprise, his foot easing on the break, slowing the truck to a crawl. 'What you did?' he said gently.

'Before. For everything to happen?' The words felt dirty and guilty when she heard them aloud.

A sadness filled Howard's eyes, crumpling his face like paper. She wished in that instant that she hadn't said it, that she'd left him out of her sordid little worry. And then, as the truck came to a standstill by the side of the road, his arm pulled her close. So close that her tears were absorbed by his shirt before they had time to fall.

'You did nothing before or after Lou. Nothing but be a good soul in the wrong place. You listen to me and you listen hard,' he said, a cool hand easing her chin up. 'Look at me,' he said as she averted her eyes.

This time she looked and all he saw was guilt.

'You are the purest thing about me and no one and nothing will see anything but that. If you go doubting yourself Lilly then we need to go reassessing this world.'

It was all she needed to hear and he was the one that needed to say it to her.

Howard lit the fires once they got into the house, partly to dry Lilly out and to make up for the morning he had spent in the pharmacy. Mr Harlow had chosen to save on heating given that the shop was closed; therefore Howard had spent most of his morning struggling with the distraction of his chattering teeth.

Lunch smelt great. Lilly had left it stewing on low heat so it would be ready to eat when they wanted it. A quick mash and it was perfect. She chose to season it to her taste, let Howard smother his in salt himself. She wolfed hers down, sitting on restlessly at the table until Howard had finished before dashing up the stairs impatiently.

'We can do the dishes later,' she called, already in her room.

'Hold on a minute Lilly Lou, I need my cigarette,' he hollered, flicking his pocket and tilting it into his mouth before gathering their bowls.

'You can smoke it out the window this once,' she shouted. 'Please, come on up — I'm dying to get started.'

He smiled at her eagerness, it reminded him of his youth, his desperation to achieve something and fast. He eased the matches out of his pocket as he climbed the stairs. He knew she'd have the window ready and waiting for him.

'What, you haven't got things started yet?' he laughed sarcastically as he entered her room to see the bed stacked with her table, chair, mirror, lights and books.

'Have that cigarette and then help me,' she grinned, twitching her toes with excitement; she had been dying to rearrange her room for weeks and only now did Howard have the time. She didn't want to wait another moment, she wanted change and she wanted it now.

17.

Change. Change is this, she thinks, noticing that she is on the pleasant side of the changing wall. She often is. She smiles, her cheeks aching from lack of movement. It didn't used to be that, pleasant; it was the opposite, the enemy. Difference has been for so long, too long. Things *are* different. She likes it here, she wants to be here more, she's accepted it. She sees it, even now, in there. Not just what she wants but what is, what is real, what she is now. It's good. Not always, she's shaking her head, it's not always good. She feels herself flail onto the cot, her head resting on something softer than the mattress – she jumps. She recognises it instantly. She knows what it is, she just hasn't seen one for a lifetime. That doesn't feel exaggerated, it really must be. She lifts her hand and cautiously strokes the surface cotton before applying pressure to feel the bounce of the stuffing. A pillow. She lifts it to the skin of her face and lets herself sink into it, all the way down to the cot until she is lying. Amazing. There is comfort in its softness. Comfort is alien, she had forgotten it. He took it away, he took everything away.

'It stinks in here,' he said, sniffing at the air, 'like piss. Did you piss in here?' His tone turning to aggression.

She had weed in the toy tea pot. It was all she could find other than a corner in the room and that she did not want to do, like some cat in its litter tray. She felt enough like an animal as it was. Groomed and trained. That would be the last straw.

'Get yourself bathed and I'll come for you shortly.'

She heaved a sigh of relief as he descended the stairs, grabbing the pot and teetering as quickly and carefully as she could toward the bathroom sink. She poured out the wee and rinsed it, placing it back before he would notice. What did he expect her to do? He had left her in there for days. She wasn't a doll. He seemed to forget sometimes.

The bathwater was cold as she stepped into it, completely cold. He hadn't attempted to make it warm. The cold tap still glistened with dew, the hot felt cold and dry to the touch – it hadn't been turned on. She bit down hard on her lip and slipped in; she wanted to be clean, she wanted washed, cold or not. She heard the creak of the stairs beneath his weight and lowered herself into the water, it seemed safer that way, she would be harder to grasp. He didn't say a word, his face was cold and blank. His hand clenched her throat and thrust her underwater. She opened her eyes to see his face through the warble as she tried to scrabble for him. It wasn't working, the view was distorted, he wasn't where she thought he was. She was thrashing around, her feet battering against the sides of the bath, sometimes the wall. He dragged her up long enough for her to gasp for breath before propelling her beneath its surface again. She got his arm and squeezed her nails into it with all her might. He cried out. She heard him through the murmur and the splashing but he didn't let go. Next time he dragged her up he got a handful of her hair and held her down twice as far.

She's writhing on the bed, wet. She can feel the wet on her skin, her clothes. His face is distorted. That's it, she can't look, she can't see it because that was it, that was the change . . .

When he dragged her out and tossed her on the cold tile floor she was spluttering for breath, water and vomit coming from her nose and mouth as she coughed up what she had inhaled.

'You wanted to leave me then. Let's see how you like me now.'

It was all a game, she thought, the dirt from his boots catching her eye on the white tile floor. He's been digging my grave. Her thoughts were manic. He left her no towel, no change of clothes. She huddled against the bath, scared to leave, waiting, waiting to see what would happen.

It was easier than this before, seeing it, living it. He was the him before, this is the him that did everything, took everything away – this is *him*. She's struggling, with herself as much as with him. She wants to look, wants to see it and have it gone, to free herself. No, no, let's just leave it. She's pulling herself back. But I have to, I did all this, came this far, I have to – then it's over. The thinking is hurting her head; she rocks it in her hands, any comfort from the pillow now gone. There is nothing when this – she thinks poking at her temples – when this is in here.

He dragged her to her feet and pulled her into the hallway. She noticed her bedroom door was closed, not just closed but the bolt at the top was pulled. He threw her a dress and trailed her to the store cupboard. Without a word he pushed her in and closed the door. He did this when he went out, she knew that, but this felt different. He hadn't let her dress, it was a struggle in such a tight space but she pulled the ill-fitting dress on and was shocked to see it dropped loosely to below her knee. It wasn't a child's dress. If it was, it was for a child much older than her. No, it was more like a woman's. She didn't care; it felt good to be wearing something that wasn't tight. Then it struck her, if it wasn't Julia's, who was she meant to be?

Why didn't he want her to be Julia anymore? She stood, in the dark, terrified.

The damp on her skin is cold. She looks between her legs – she's wet herself. It's been so long. She glances to the toilet cubicle and feels ashamed. She had thought that was over. See what he does! She can't see him without something like this. She stands, not looking at them by their table, hoping they won't see her. Silly, she knows they will. She makes it to the toilet and drags her dress over her head; her pants already kicked off, she sits on the seat. She feels sticky; she's hoping the air will change that. There's movement beyond the door, she hears the shuffle of feet, the muffle of voices. She could hear what they were saying if she tried but she doesn't want to, they're not in her world; they're here, not in there. She wants back in there. That's enough for one day. She's seen enough. She knows what happens next, she knows where she goes.

★

She cried. She cried a lot, or so it seemed, but it was his first experience of a baby. They said she was good, settled in her ways; he struggled to see it. To be honest, he never really cared. All he noticed were the two extremes – peace or crying, either way she was just Baby Lila.

It was a Tuesday night. He remembers because he had been at school and the day before was Monday, the first day after the weekend, always the hardest. This was Tuesday. It wasn't strange to hear the crying through the night, he was getting used to it; it had been six weeks of dirty nappies, crying and havoc. The rest of the family were taking it all in their stride; after all, he had been the last baby all those five years earlier. He was proud to no longer be the youngest, he felt like one of the boys overnight. He saw the two teams, girls and boys, the littlest member being a girl; that made their side weaker. She hadn't been crying too long but he thought he would try to comfort her before his parents woke up, especially his mother. She was feeling the strain, he could tell by the weepiness. Either that or she was losing her edge. Pa and Suzie blamed it on hormones, the things women have when they have babies – makes them cry a lot. A good night's sleep was sure to help.

Lila was still sleeping in the crib Pa had set up by their bed. It sat on the side nearest the door, making it easier for him to reach, which was why the noise spread into the house so much. It was dark, made him assume it was the middle of the night. It was in fact just after ten but all were tucked up in bed for the night. His eyes had adjusted to the dark by the time he negotiated his way down the hall. It was a slow process, tiny steps so as to avoid tripping on some toy left strewn on the floor. They were bad like that, leaving a mess. Ma would usually have them all cleared away after lights out but she wasn't doing things quite the same at the moment; he put that down to being so busy with Lila.

He made it to her bedside without a hitch. She was crying. Not manically, not a boob cry as Ma called it – it was more like the one she did when she wanted to settle. There wasn't much to look at, wrinkly skin and a big mouth. She barely had hair. He had had lots apparently, when he came out, a big shock of black hair, like a monkey. She was bald, like an old man. He had settled her a few times before now, during the day but it's all the same; wrap her tight, drop the blanket over her face and voila, peace. She was funny like that, wouldn't sleep without the blanket over her face and it wouldn't do to just have it a little bit over, no, it had to be right across her face or it fell off when she wriggled and then she started up all over again. Ma wasn't at all keen on her wanting it like that, but she had tried to break the habit to no avail.

'Whatever works,' she had said.

No wonder she was crying, he thought, her tiny arms and legs flailing in the air, free from any restriction; she would hate that. He felt for the far corner of the blanket and pulled it tight across her chest, tucking it in behind her back. He did the same with the other side, keeping it slightly looser this time, if one side was tight, it should do. Wouldn't be good to have her completely bound. Then he gathered a little of the loose material and draped it over her face. She was quiet already. He smiled, pleased with himself. Glancing over the bed he saw both parents fast asleep – his father's snoring confirmed it. He stroked her head before leaving; he wanted to, he loved her. Strange, he thought, loving this wee annoying thing. He should have no reason to but he just can't help it, she's lovely. His walk back to bed was speedier, he could see by now and he knew which parts of his path were obstructed. He made it back unheard.

The shrill cry startled him, waking him from what had been a pleasant, unbroken sleep. He knew instantly it was Ma. He knew the moment he realised he was awake, perhaps he even knew before that. He flew out of bed so fast that he caught himself on the duvet and tripped on his way out the door before charging up the hall. Suzie and Stan were already there. Ethan crashed in close behind Tommy. She was on the bed, sobbing uncontrollably, frantically rocking Lila in her arms. She looked at them, eyes red and sore, skin blotchy and marbled like he had never seen it before. She had been crying longer than the time it had taken him to get there. She had been crying a lot longer. She squeezed Lila tight to her chest and struggled for breath – she had no intention of telling them what was wrong, it took their father to step forward. He too had been crying. Tommy stared more closely. He had never seen his father's eyes so transparent; they were glistening, a shade of turquoise.

'Kids, it's little . . .' He choked on the words and spluttered a number of unintelligible grunts before gathering himself, fist pressed hard against his lips as he spoke as if to control them from giving up again. 'Little Lila's not with us any longer. She's passed on.' He struggled to stand and instead collapsed back onto the bed at a distance from Ma and the baby.

They all stood, open-mouthed in shock. Suzie was the first to respond; she fell at her mother's feet and wept. The boys, the boys were different. They didn't quite know what to do with themselves. Stan ran away, it was all he could do to cope with the news. Tommy didn't notice Ethan, or what he did, he was too busy staring at his Ma. He had never seen such pain, he had never seen any to be honest and this was extreme. There was something very alive in her suffering. He could see it move inside her, there was a beauty to it. He opened his mouth to confess but nothing came out, he was empty, muted by the pain. She stared up at him with begging eyes and waited for him speak but all he could do was breathe. He didn't take the chance, he couldn't. He wouldn't have known what to say if he had. Instead he watched the weight of guilt fall on her shoulders as she slumped beneath it, giving in. He saw and said nothing. He didn't know how. He was struggling – with what had happened, what he'd done. It was all too much. He just didn't get the chance to say anything.

Two months she stayed in bed after Lila's death. Two solid months. In that time their father took on both roles: his own and their mother's. They didn't mind at first, it seemed understandable for her to remove herself from them to cope with her pain, but they witnessed it change to self-absorption and loathing. Loathing of herself and her husband. They saw her repulsion at his existence and began to hate her for it; he was only a man, after all, and every man has his failings.

He cooked, cleaned, washed and bathed them. Suzie did what she could but she was too young back then to be of much greater use – she was only nine. It was hard, hard for them all to have an absent mother, harder still to see the grassless mound beyond the back of the house every time they stepped outside.

Tommy witnessed, at different times, that they had all been affected by it. For them, it was no greater than pain, but he was assigned a more potent concoction – that of pain and guilt. It stung in his chest. He wanted to cry out and let them all know, but time was making it harder. He went once, to the wood, and bellowed it out, screamed it at the top of his voice. It felt good, great in fact, in that moment, the freedom, the ease of having said it. But it didn't last. The gates shut fast and he was yet again locked away with his confession. He wasn't the only one suffering in silence; they all were, some more than others.

He caught his father the odd time, crying. He knew his father's ways and he knew better than to let him know he'd seen. Instead, he just gazed at his back, the gentle shudders comforted by the bottle of whisky in his hand, slurping between staggered breaths.

Pa cried all right. To himself, it would always be to himself; he wouldn't like the kids to see it, see that he had weakness, that he was as human as them. It would be worse still if his wife ever heard, thought he wasn't coping, thought he was a sad excuse for a supportive husband and father. That's what she would think, he knew it. He knew it and showed her nothing but strength, strength under every circumstance, even if it killed him. It did in the end, that and the utter lapse in communication. It was the wrong decision of a man so unaware of his own capabilities and his own demons. He chose to protect them by drowning himself; instead he alienated them and signed their pact with despair, every last name on the dotted line, with Tommy at the forefront. He wasn't to know. Tommy liked the weakness, if ever he caught a glimpse of it. It was endearing, a comfort to see they weren't alone in their struggle. It felt that way a lot. Each pretending for the sake of the others that everything was all right, even when it came to Ma, pretending she would be okay, forever reassuring one another. They all felt differently, knew it was a lie, they just chose not to voice it. Keeping things positive for the sake of the next person. How wrong they had been. It was the way of the family, the dynamic they were learning from one another with each passing day, how to behave, how to respond. But someone was bound to crack, someone had to break, they just never thought it would be him – Pa.

The drinking didn't become noticeable for a year or so. It was under control at first, just a tipple at the end of the day, but it didn't stay that way for long. Mother tried to take control the odd time. When she was up and about she would be nice, act caring toward him for the sake of the kids, but this just made matters worse. He didn't want false shows of affection, he wanted the real deal. He wanted a wife that wanted him and he wasn't going to find that here. He never strayed, wouldn't have had it in him, he was too much in love with her to consider looking elsewhere. No, his mistress was the bottle and she was fast winning his affections.

Tommy wasn't totally aware of the goings on. He thought things were okay between his parents, okay enough that they might make another baby and put things right. He had heard the doctor say that, he said, 'It would be advised to help deal with the grief,' but as the years rolled in, he realised it would never be a reality.

It came to him a few times over the first couple of years to tell his Ma what he had done, that it was all his fault and not hers, that he was to blame for the death of little Lila. But he never could find the right moment.

He would go to her full of good intentions and then something would stop him. If she was nice he soaked it up like a sponge. He seldom had a mother, a real one, but when she was there she was fabulous. She would show him how to bake, tell him stories of monsters in the woods; it was too good to jeopardise by raking the whole thing up again. She had so few days free from it. Then there were the dark days, the ones that stole her from him, from them all, and kept her locked away. He could see it in her eyes, the shadow that fell behind them, that's where it kept her. The darkness, that's where it locked her. Sometimes he thought it would be easier to tell her like that but the chill in the room forced him to change his mind. She was too cold and distant to understand, she scared him like that, made him question what she would do. No, it just never seemed suitable.

By the age of eight he gave up ever saying anything about it and started to forget, but it didn't last long. It was then time to witness his father's descent. He blamed himself for that too. He knew it was all because of Lila and Lila was because of him. Be it because his mother was laid up – that was his fault. Be it because Pa couldn't cope with raising the kids – that was his fault. Be it that he was becoming a dribbling, bloated mess – that was his fault. He saw himself in everything, from every direction, but who ever said, 'Tommy, you killed your sister'? He did. He said it to himself every day for two years and every day for the months before Pa died. He had ruined everything.

That was his guilty secret. That was why she was coming for him, and she was going to get him.

His father had taught him about knot-tying. How ironic. He was the cause of his father's death and now his father would play a hand in his. He sniggered; it was funny.

He heard the crack as the air soared between his toes. He heard the crack and that was it.

It was over.

18.

She shoots bolt upright – she can see everything.

The wood, Thickets Wood, it is *him*.

He is Mrs Christmas Eve.

Her body wanes and flops against the pillow of the cot.

She sees.

The inexplicable force of fear inside her is *him*. He is it – he is theirs too. He has to be.

The woods and their secrets are a manifestation of *him*. She let him in there; she opened the doors and let *him* in. She had seen it, earlier, a little. She had seen the dark brought on by reliving, but she had never seen so clearly its effect. He is her unchartered fear but they are her solitude, always have been and now he's got to them, made things as dark for them as they are for her.

She knows herself better than she ever thought. She can see it so clearly now. For the first time everything makes sense.

Her grandmother is Tommy's mother.

Her grandfather was his father. The man whose love and devotion was ruined by the self-indulgent woman in his life.

She isn't just Lilly. She's Tommy.

She's more Tommy than anyone.

Lilly is who she wanted to be, who she could have been, but Tommy, he is her. He's her now, this moment, this time. His fears are her fears, a projection of everything she had fought so hard to forget. Until now, until recently, until they, they started making her look at it, look at *him*. She can see it; she put Tommy there, through that, in her own little world as a result of everything she's been looking at.

Her memories have caused Tommy's stress.

She isn't happy.

She wants *him* out.

She knows she has to do it; she has to look. She curls into a ball and clasps her sheet close to her face. It's crisp from the heat. She smiles; it reminds her she's warm. It takes all her energy to drag herself off the cot and scuttle into the adjoining room. The mattress is warm to the touch, too warm but she lies on it anyway. She has to do this. Her eyes close.

It was a car journey, she knew because he told her beforehand.

It scared her at first when he pulled her from her bed. No warning, just dark, pitch dark before he bagged her head and threw her into the boot. The prospect of her future was exciting, even his forcefulness didn't worry her.

She had hope.

Her natural assumption was that he was giving her away. Anything more sinister didn't occur to her. It wouldn't have, she was too young, too innocent to comprehend what was ahead. It was naivety, she knows that now.

His car boot was clean, unlike the other man's; it smelt like new upholstery and plastic, which was fitting, as he was meticulous. Beneath her rustled when she moved, like she was lying on bags. They were the cause of the smell, sniffing confirmed it. He had said she contaminated things; maybe it was his way of keeping the boot clean.

It was a short walk between the car and where he brought her, much like when she came to him. Short enough for him to have walked her up a driveway. She should have been so lucky.

This was the first time she saw it.

It was much like this. She opens her eyes and drops her head toward the body of the room. There is little difference. Everything is duplicated; she knows that now. It's not real, not really.

It was nothing more than a concrete shell with a bed made in the corner with a sheet and duvet. The overturned bucket opposite the door meant nothing to her at first. She just assumed it had been left there for no particular reason.

Her focus falls on the rusting bucket opposite. She was a quick learner.

She stood close to the bed, his hand clutching her arm as he kicked the door closed behind him. He released his hold and lingered. He was uncomfortable; she knew by the way he hovered, inspecting the room. He was silent, as was she. The keys hung limp on the chain beneath his knee, they swung as he moved; she chose to watch them rather than him. They were inanimate, inconsequential; that made them soothing. He was making her anxious. He rubbed the palms of his hands on the front of his sweater, they were sweaty, she had felt the dampness in his grip. He paced around, lifting the bucket, running his hand along the duvet to satisfy himself.

'You'll be okay here, won't you? Enough to keep you going I think,' he said. She could hear a doubt in his questioning. She didn't understand. He rubbed his hands again in exactly the same spot; they hung by his sides now, all fingers twitching.

'Right.'

He pulled the door closed; the click rang in her ears. It's ringing now. Loud and clear. That was it – she was home.

The frantic rubbing of her ears made them burn, they're hot to the touch. She chooses instead to stroke them gently, her apology for being so hard on them. She had wanted the ringing to stop, it has worked. Over, she thinks. Over. It's over. I'm here; it's not real. Her chest lightens as she exhales. She wants to forget again, just for now. Peace. A little place of peace.

★

'Tommy,' she called.

'Tommy.'

The sound reverberated off the trees; it was Stan.

'Tommy, you here?' She was calm, no panic in her voice; this took effort.

She focused on the egg that lay nestled in her palm, its shell warm. She spun it, her fingers crooked to keep it from falling, her thumb working it in rotation.

'Tommy.'

She had been making omelettes. The cheese would be hardening. She had left it uncovered.

'Tommy.' She turned to the cry on her left and called out, this time not to Tommy, to Stan. 'Where can he be?'

'He'll be here, don't worry.'

Four rotations, five rotations, six rotations . . .

Stan seemed effortlessly calm. That was partially her doing, she assumed, keeping her nerves so well constrained.

The shell was smooth. No impurities, she thought, an example of perfection so seldom seen in life. She glanced around, her eyes straining in the fading light; he was nowhere.

'Tommy.' Her voice cracked slightly. She felt it and coughed in an attempt to disguise it.

She began rotating with her fingers rather than her thumb; it was more difficult, more of a distraction.

'Tommy, please, it's getting dark. Tommy?'

There was questioning in her tone, as though she wondered who she was talking to, if anyone at all. Fear was creeping in, she could feel it, little by little, niggling at her. It took every ounce of her focus to keep it at bay. She knew fear. It knew her, and well. Old friends, she thought, the leaves damp beneath her feet as she trudged deeper into the undergrowth of the wood. She stifled a laugh; she and fear went way back – seven years, more.

'Tommy, I don't know what you're playing at but this isn't funny anymore,' Stan yelled, his concern over the last few days turning to bitterness. He was lost in all this, hadn't a clue what to do. 'Sorry,' he cried, 'I didn't mean to get cross, I'm just worried about you.' He thudded on, eyes peeled. He was beginning to feel like a pillock talking to nothing more than trees and the distant voice of his mother.

'Tom . . . my,' she called slowly, triggering her memory of the rhyme. It began creeping to the forefront of her mind. Now fear truly had set in. She could feel herself beginning to panic; one rotations, two rotations, three rotat . . . its crack rang in her ears as the ground split its shell. She was standing, full stretch when she glanced down to see the yolk and white mingling with the undergrowth, his shadow casting darkness on its sheen. What a pretty egg it had been. She didn't feel herself fall, only the twigs stabbing her hands made her aware of it. She cried out uncontrollably. Her shriek cut through the silence of the wood like an animal, her pain was intolerable – in that second it was bitterly raw.

Stan heard and followed the sound. His mother was nowhere

in sight – they had both wandered, gone their separate ways – but he was gaining distance. His feet pounding hard on the dirt as he charged toward her cry. His mind ran in tangents. Had she fallen, been attacked, bitten? Nothing could have prepared him for the truth. When he saw Tommy, he skidded to a stop. He didn't believe it for the first second; in the next, he scaled the tree and grabbed out for him as soon as he thought his arm would stretch. He had been deceived. His fingers grazed Tommy's trousers but he was too far out. Stan climbed higher until he reached the branch behind Tommy and seized his arm. It was cold, shocking him into letting go. This only sent him into a swing, Stan had to wait, time his next attempt to get him. This time he managed it, dragging the dead weight onto the branch, the rope limp as he tugged it free from Tommy's neck.

Ma stayed kneeling in the dirt, the damp seeping into her skin as she stared up at his dirty soles. All ten toes grubby with soil. Ten little toes, the same ten little toes she had so loved when he was little. She pushed herself to her feet, the eggshell crunching beneath her weight as she forced her knees hard into the dirt. It was crushed; ironic, she thought. She only got half way up before slumping into the tree. It was then she felt the etching.

'Ma, Ma,' spluttered Stan, 'you have to get Suzie.'

She stepped back and saw the trunk clearly for the first time; he had etched into it, he had scarred it with the rhyme.

'Ma, I can't get him down.' Stan was becoming hysterical.

She stood, gazing up at her boys. She had been trying so hard these past few days. It was too little too late, she knew that now. They were her boys, she thought, her precious, perfect boys.

She had gotten up just two days before. It had been the first time in three weeks that she had left her room for more than a bathroom run, but Suzie had begged.

'Ma, I can't do it,' she said, quite composed. 'First he said he was sick, then he stopped eating, now he's seeing all kinds in his room. I don't know what else to do!' The composure was gone; her voice cracked and tears filled the rift.

It wasn't like Suzie to come to her with anything regarding the family. She was a warrior, took things on and dealt with them, keeping any signs of upset or distress clear from her mother's view, but this was too big. She had hit a brick wall and she needed someone older, wiser to try and deal with it. She thought perhaps they were linked, her mother's ailing ways and Tommy, thought maybe it was an inherited weakness, one she herself could not relate to.

'I know, what with Pa, that you need peace and I honestly wouldn't come to you unless I couldn't do it. Even had Miss Margaret and the church round trying to help us out, seeing Tommy being all wayward. I think we need to do something about it. I'm starting to crack under this pressure and I don't want people thinking I can't, we can't cope.'

'I had no idea he was in such a mess. I thought he was a little more upset than you others but I thought he'd be over it by now,' she said, trying to muster some form of concern.

'So did I. He's terrible, he's gone, I don't know how to talk to him anymore. He's just gone,' Suzie cried, her emotions getting the better of her.

'Okay, don't you worry I'll be up and about in five minutes,' she smiled, a warm hand on her daughter's shoulder. She lied; she lied through her teeth to give Suzie some shred of hope. She was no more capable of being around them all now than she had been all those weeks ago. She would do her best but there was no guaranteeing anything.

Tommy was in his room keeping himself to himself when he heard her come in. It was his mother, he knew by the smell of perfume that filled the room ahead of her. He didn't want to see her, didn't want to see anyone and the fact she was here meant Suzie had told her there was something up. There was something up all right, something none of them could help with. He watched the window from the corner of the closet. He had chosen to spend his time there recently because it was the darkest part of the room come nightfall. If he were in it he could be sure no one else was. It had been his biggest dread and he was proud to have overcome it.

'Tommy?' she cooed encouragingly. 'Tomm . . . oh there you are,' she had caught sight of him in the corner of her eye. He looked at her for the first time in weeks. She was slimmer than he remembered, and taller; the one contributed to the other. Her cheeks had more colour than in past years and her step more bounce. She was doing a great job of pretending, he thought. She knelt down to his level and sat hunkered in front of him. This made him uneasy, blocked his view of the room and to make matters worse, she had left the door open.

'I think we need a chat,' she smiled.

He didn't need to chat. No amount of chatting was going to change anything – anything then, anything now. No, he didn't need to chat, she did. What he needed was peace. To be left alone. He needed to watch what *she* did, the things *she* brought. He needed to keep track, not miss anything. Ma, just like Suzie, wouldn't possibly understand that.

'Suzie tells me you're not coping very well, that you're conjuring up all kinds in here,' she said, tapping at her temple.

Her eyes were grey, a marble shade of grey, he had noticed that not long after the death of his sister. There was always a weight behind her stare, an emptiness that made them appear cold and distant. He blamed himself for that. For taking the love from her eyes.

'I think you need to just snap out of it and come out of here.' Her hand was on his arm, not hard but tugging at him gently, encouraging him to move without force; it wasn't working.

'Tommy, please don't make me fight you.'

He was going to, whether she was up to it or not. It was survival of the fittest in here and he wasn't going anywhere.

She held onto his arms and pulled, all the time questioning if this was the right approach. How would she know? Part of her knew it was selfishness that had made her take this line of action. She wanted to shake him out of it so she could go back to her room, shut them all out and continue to forget. A small part of her resented him for putting her in this situation and didn't mind if he got hurt in the process.

'Tommy, I will get you out of here one way or another,' she said, loosening her grip and sending him flailing against the wall. She jumped to her feet and strode toward the window. The curtains were drawn, but the air was stuffy, it couldn't be good, she thought as she opened the window. It was just a slither but Tommy charged at her from where he sat, darted toward the window like a bull and slammed it shut, sending her falling against it in the process.

'It stays shut!' he barked. He saw it, in that second he saw the black air creep in. It had been waiting, waiting for days. Stupid woman, she was much better off just leaving them alone.

'That's it, you are out of here,' she said, her grip now so tight on his arm he could feel the pinch of her nails. 'No excuses, I want you out and about. You need to snap out of this!'

He had scared her, she had no idea things were so bad.

She got him as far as the kitchen. It was an improvement, she knew that much by the joy on Suzie's face, but it was short lived.

'Stop twitching, you look weird,' Ethan said when he came back from school. Tommy didn't say a word, he hadn't spoken all day.

'He's acting a bit strange, you sure we shouldn't send for someone?' Stan whispered in Suzie's ear, his eyes watching Tommy as he sat on the stool close to the stove, his eyes darting from place to place, arms frantically rubbing to keep himself warm.

'No, it's a process. I think.' She was as uncertain as he was.

He stayed there until his mother ushered him to bed. It felt better. Not much; he was all alone in the room he had once made safe. It wasn't safe any longer, it had been left open all day, exposed.

The next day came fast; he had slept in spite of himself.

'Tommy, we need sticks for drying out, you wouldn't be a pet and go collect some please?' his mother called through the door she had already opened in passing.

It wasn't a question; it was an order put politely. He couldn't go out, he knew he couldn't; he remembered what happened last time. She was there, waiting for him.

'Do as I ask please,' she said, peering through the doorway. He was beginning to despise her.

The woods were gloomy, he saw that on his approach, knew as much. It was November after all, what else would he expect? Sticks. Sticks weren't hard to find, he thought, his toe nearing the first throng of trees. The air was cold, freezing even as he entered.

He could hear the crackling of branches in the breeze, the swoosh overhead. He searched for comfort in it but only found fear. He was filled with it, had been since he left the house. It was strong, stronger than when he sat in his room and waited; he was tempting her and he knew it, teasing *her* to get him. This was *her* playground after all, not his. This was all about *her* and this was where she won. Thickets Wood.

He stumbled as his toe caught on a root, sending him headlong into the dirt and leaves. From nowhere they appeared, the moths. He batted out as they swarmed around his head, their hum so loud in his ears he couldn't think straight. He fumbled for the few sticks he had gathered; they were strewn around his knees. He would get them and get out. He had to get out.

Suzie was on the hill outside their house, watching, waiting for him to return. She was worried, she remembered the result of his last errand. She wasn't sure who it was at first, if it was a person at all when he came flailing up the hill, frantically batting out at himself and the air around him. He was attacking something, she just couldn't see what. It was only as he neared that she realised there was nothing, he was beating the air, his hands over his ears when he took a second's ease. His face was strained, twisting and contorting as though frantically trying to shake something.

She watched him, uncertain what to do, how to respond. It was shock that took over more than anything; she was numb to it and getting used to feeling that way. She stood, motionless and watched as he calmed, gathering himself and the sticks he had pushed into his back pocket – it must have been no more than three but he had them and was proud. Ma wouldn't be impressed. Suzie didn't care; right now she just wanted him home. The mother in her flared up, the furnace of movement relit by the fear she felt for him. She could hear him as he neared, singing. It made her smile, it was a sign of hope. It wasn't until she ran to meet him that her smile faded.

Tommy went into the woods today,
Tommy Tinkit lost his way.
Tommy went into the woods today,
Tommy Tinkit went astray.
Tommy went into the woods today,
Tommy Tinkit's darkest day.

She stood before him and listened because that was all she knew how to do.

Tommy went into the woods today,
Tommy Tinkit lost his way.
Tommy went into the woods today,
Tommy Tinkit went astray.
Tommy went into the woods today,
Tommy Tinkit's darkest day.

He didn't acknowledge her as he wandered past, she wasn't even sure he saw her. He went as far as the fence marking their grounds and began stacking the sticks against it; he set them up, then restacked them and moved them along a little, continuing in this way until he had covered most of the front patch. A tear fell down her cheek. Poor Tommy, what were they going to do with him? She was quick to sweep it away as she saw her mother approach from inside the house. It wouldn't do to show any kind of weakness around her, she had to believe she was strong, strong enough to rear this lot. She glanced back down at Tommy and wondered for the first time if she was.

'That's not going to do much,' Ma said, her hands frantically working a dishcloth around the edge of a plate. 'What the hell were you doing out there so long?' she added with a giggle before pausing, awestruck. He had now moved to alongside the dog pen, three sticks in hand, stacking and restacking his way along.

Tommy went into the woods today,
Tommy Tinkit lost his way.
Tommy went into the woods today,
Tommy Tinkit went astray.
Tommy went into the woods today,
Tommy Tinkit's darkest day.

She was numbed to hear him, see him so distant. 'Tom boy?' It had been years since she called him that but it came to her and she wanted to, she wanted that link; that grasp at closeness. 'Tommy, you hear me?' she asked, a flicker of panic crossing her face.

'Stan! Stan!' she bellowed in distress.

She had never meant for this, she had thought he would just snap out of it. How wrong she had been.

Stan stumbled out of the door, his glass of milk slopping over the edge as he drew to a stop against the frame. 'What you . . .' He paused, Tommy's actions drawing his attention.

'Tommy?' he said, thrusting the glass into his mother's hand, the contents continuing to slosh over the edge, unnoticed. 'Tommy!' he called, by now both hands gripping his little brother's arms, shaking him violently in an attempt to bring him round. 'Tommy stop it, talk to me.'

He continued chanting, his stare blank. He was looking right through them.

'What is he saying?' Ma cried. 'Why is he saying all this?'

She looked up from the etched rhyme in the trunk and wondered what could have been so bad? This Mrs Christmas Eve. She smiled. Well, you got the better of her, at least you have that comfort my boy; she can't ever get to you now. The stab to her heart was greater than that of losing baby Lila, much greater. She realised that only now, in losing her boy – what she had done to them, to all of them. She had walked through the valley of sworn evil every day since her daughter died and now she had been the force to let another of her young slip through her fingers. She was more the devil than she knew. She followed her glance and saw his grubby soles, strewn and misshapen in whatever form Stan could keep a grip of him. He was twelve and he was dead. She had said it, if only to herself – he was dead. The strength of the myth lies only with the believer.

19.

She's sitting on the cot, both feet swinging through the air. It's nice. She's smiling. It reminds her of freedom. Her arms stretch above her head – it's gone, it's over. She feels free; this feels free.

She pushes herself to her feet and walks into the adjoining room. The handle is cold to the touch. She has seen it before but never touched it. She hadn't wanted to. She wants to now. She grasps it and pulls hard to release it from the wall. It doesn't budge. She glances down and sees the plastic wedged beneath the bottom. She kicks at it with her foot. It's not a hard kick; it hurts her toes too much. It holds fast. She tries again, this time her weight pushing against the door, freeing it accidently to fire across the floor. She gazes at it until it rests against the toilet wall. The door is heavy, alarmingly so, pushing against her as it closes. She jumps free of its path into the changing room and smiles at the click. It's closed. It's gone. She can still hear it in her ears.

Click.

She likes it, it means closure, it means 'move on'.

She stands, eyes squeezed tightly shut, and thinks of them. She needs them, needs Thatchbury. It's her safe place, even still. She can't be without them and he can't be there. She feels for it. It's there, always will be.

Thickets Wood.

Mrs Christmas Eve.

No, the darkness is gone. This time, for now at least. She can see it, see the pattern. She knows she does it, brings them places and brings things to them. She can't help it; they're in there, in the jumble of everything in her head. Her mind isn't a nice place, not truly. It can't be. She couldn't make it that way. It is what it is. It is Thatchbury, her way. Howard and Lilly, that's all she ever searched for, that was all she ever wanted.

She looks down at the girl from where she's standing at the opposing end of the room; the sight never fails to weaken her in some way. She's momentarily shocked; she hadn't expected such progress so quickly. The nurses sitting at their post glance round at her with similarly shocked expressions. The door in question had been open for six months, never touched, most certainly never closed.

Lilly Doe. They call her Doe because they have no trace of her surname; she has given them numerous ones over the sessions in the last six months but their records show she does not fall under any of them. She is twenty-three or thereabouts, with the appearance of a girl half that age. Stooped and frail, her bones are barely covered. Her stoop is not medically inflicted, more a result of being cooped up, long periods in tight spaces. With the stoop she is only around five foot two inches, four inches shorter than her measured height. Gives the illusion of a child. Her hair is thick and dark. They have not ventured to wash it so it shines in grease and there are traces of dandruff from her incessant scratching. She scratches a lot; it is one of her releases, a vice they cannot seem to infiltrate. Her teeth are nothing short of a mess. A number of the front six are heavily ridged, with clustered teeth piling in behind on the right-hand side. They had wondered about the cause but the tooth bar explained it. What inhumanity, she thought, flinching at the notion. Her skin is a sickly shade of white brought on from fourteen years in captivity, it's ghostlike. The dark circles beneath her eyes show up heavy in contrast. They are a combination of darkness, malnutrition and possibly a birth trait, it would be hard to tell. The floral print dress hangs just short of her knees to reveal two scars they have not yet found the source of. Perhaps with time. From what she's heard of him it could be anything; he seemed to have little regard for the pain he inflicted. She is uncomfortable to look at. An uneasiness goes with her appearance, and a vacant stare that makes being in her presence strained.

This room is her solitude, she thinks, glancing around the facility. A safe place, especially now that she has shut the door on the replica room; that is a real breakthrough. She may not progress much further regarding her living space, but with time they'll introduce comforts, like the pillow. She checks the report hanging from the file in her arm; it went down well she sees. That is progress. She ponders for a moment considering the next appropriate thing to introduce. Flicking back through the session notes, one thing jumps out – cutlery. Not metal as they were using before she was aware of the tooth bar, but plastic. She scribbles a reminder on the notepad resting on top of the file. 'Inform kitchen to use plastic. Spoons only.' That would be a fantastic step in the right direction if she took to it.

She smiles in Lilly's direction; she is sitting curled against the wall, her tatty sheet draped across her knees, eyes closed. She'll be in her safe place she assumes, motioning to Nurse Patterson to follow her outside. She had mentioned going away, in her head, a few times. It seems a natural pattern in captivity cases and this seems healthy – no signs of schizophrenia or personality loss. She continues to study her as the nurse stands patiently by the door. She knows the routine practice of a doctor call: no unnecessary door closing or disruption; she must wait before going outside to be given an update on treatment.

Dr Martin turns abruptly on her heel and strides through the door, closely followed by Nurse Patterson.

'What have your observations been over this past week?' Dr Martin asks, an air of impatience in her tone.

'Nothing other than what's stated in the file.'

Dr Martin cuts her short. 'I can see what's in the file. I just want you to give me a brief rundown of how she's been, how she seems.'

Nurse Patterson pauses for a thought. 'Things have been good. She had the one incident of opening her bladder on herself but that was related to the therapy session so it is altogether a different matter to how things used to be. She's been moving around a little more, using the toilet, eating the food. We're really pleased. She is no closer to interaction but she seems to fear our presence a little less. She even looked at Davis.'

'Now that's why I prefer you to articulate things rather than simply have me read all the paperwork,' she says with a smile. 'It creates a much clearer picture.' She licks her finger and leafs through the file. 'It says here that she accepted a change of clothing? I gathered that by looking at her but there was no problem?' she asks sceptically.

'It took a few hours for her to do it but no, no problem at all.'

Dr Martin smiles. She had taken a gamble in her approach to the therapy, choosing to take her back and relive the events running up to the captivity but it seems to have paid off. She is improving more now than in the six months she spent isolated in the replica, terrified of acceptance or change. Now she has prospect of living a vaguely acceptable life. She wouldn't go so far as to refer to it as normal, she imagined it would never be that. But then again, she could be wrong – she hoped to be. That would be incredible progress for such a case.

'Dr Martin, are there any changes to be made or do we remain as we are?' Nurse Patterson's voice broke her thoughts.

'Sorry, Patterson, no, no changes. I think if we just continue as we are, little by little we'll keep moving forward. Every little counts.' She grins. She steps aside, allowing Nurse Patterson to access the door handle and re-enter Lilly's room. The close of the door is almost silent, the click so low she imagines Lilly will have remained unaware of it. She smiles, this pleases her.

She removes her notepad and lets it fall into the deep pocket of her white coat before hanging the file on the hook close to the door frame. She double-checks the name on the file with the door. This is more habit than necessity but she does it all the same.

'Lilly Doe – 16 A/B'

She is hanging the file beside the door marked 'Lilly Doe 16 B'. She will no longer be using door 'A', thanks to Lilly, thanks to progress. That should be her second name, she smiles to herself, Georgina Progress Martin. But it doesn't quite work like Georgina Cherry Martin. She grins again. This time slyness curls up the edges rather than gratification. Progress means nothing beside Cherry. Cherry and Ivan mean a lot.

Cherry Tree

Part Three of the Thickets Wood Trilogy

Rebecca Reid

1.

It had been one of those days. Typical, nothing alarming in any way. Then Lilly comes to mind, popping into the forefront as patients tend to do when they make progress, and she is flashing her sign like mad for attention right now. She will indulge it, she has the time, she thinks, fingering a Marlboro free of the box and slipping it into her mouth. Lilly is her main patient for the moment. She knows that will change now that she is moving steadily forward, but right now she is it and things are going swimmingly.

The smoke is hot in her throat as she draws on the butt for her second hit of nicotine; it is well overdue. It is a cold autumn day, colder than she had first realised. Having spent most of her day indoors, she is feeling the chill more than usual and thinks perhaps she would be better off inside the car rather than leaning against it. She gathers her coat around herself and slips inside. Better put the window down, she thinks, starting the engine, the low hum of the radio filtering in. She doesn't want the window down but she can't go home smelling like a human ashtray either, she'd never hear the end of it. Despite the cold she puts it down to its limit and hangs her Marlboro-laden hand out into the evening air. The trees are pretty; a momentary distraction from Lilly as she focuses on their circus of colours. They are fabulous. She smiles, thinking of Lilly and how much she's missing sadden her. Taking another draw on the cigarette, she opens the crisps lying discarded on the passenger seat. Cheese and onion; she rolls her eyes. Not the best for speaking up close to people. She's glad she left them this morning, given the emergency meeting that forced her into close proximity with Doctor Newell. She pops the first crisp into her mouth. The flavor buzzes on her tongue, mingling with the taste of smoke.

Water, she thinks, scavenging around. Her water bottle is a trusty friend; she's been using the same one for months now, taking it home and rinsing it out each night. He is constant and non-intrusive; he's the closest thing she has to a stable relationship. Any kind of stability really, other than her career. That box is ticked. She fumbles around the floor below the passenger seat, head thrust onto the base, outstretched arm clinging to the steering wheel – bingo – the ridged lid grazes her finger. She struggles for a second longer before dragging it onto her knee and pulling herself up. How undignified, she thinks, had she been seen. It's a little dirty, mainly gravel, but she sweeps it away and glugs down the contents.

She feels a draft through the open window and realises why. She winds the window up, wondering why she hadn't thought to do it as soon as she tossed the butt. She shakes it off, it's done now. Bloody well cold though. She twists the heat to max and closes all the vents, waiting for the darn thing to warm up. Nothing worse than having cold air blast in. She never can understand people who endure the cold while waiting for the engine to heat – it seems so witless. She smiles knowing she knows better and feeling good about the thought that others are silly and mindless enough not to realise these things. She likes that, the thought of others' inadequacies.

Home is a twenty-minute drive. She uses this time to unwind. There's little other opportunity; this is it, between closing one door and opening another. She doesn't want to think as far ahead as opening another. No, that time would come soon enough. For now, she wants to focus on this. The moment, the peace, the music. Music is her release. It never used to be but it is now, lets her forget her own life and be absorbed in someone else's. It's indulgent and intoxicating; she likes that. There was another thing she cherished about the drive home: the opportunity to be alone. It would mean nothing to some people, they wouldn't even notice it, in fact. But she did. She noticed and she longed for it. She longed for independence. To be liberated. People didn't understand and those that pretended to just thought she was a bitch. Deep down she knew it. She could see it behind their eyes when they smiled and nodded at what she said. She wasn't a bitch, though. She was human. That is one thing about the job; she sees the differences between pretense and bona fide character traits. She doesn't pretend, doesn't say what wants to be heard. She tells the truth, says it as it is. She wished other people did that more often. Her fingers tighten on the steering wheel; she wished they were less phony. There were times when she wondered if she were being unfair, but that weakness has passed, she thinks. She wouldn't be swayed by other people's imaginings of how they would be or what they would do. They had no idea. She was the one living it, so she was the one who knew what they were talking about; it was from experience after all.

She's remembering yesterday's argument with Rupert, her elder brother. She fumbles for the glovebox and pulls an unopened box of Marlboros up to her mouth, biting at the plastic and tearing away the bronze foil to get at the cigarettes. The smell of a new packet excites her; she can feel her heart race at the thought of the nicotine. She blindly pulls one free and, tossing the packet back into the glovebox, lifts the lighter from the cup-holder and lights the tip. The burn smells almost as good as it tastes. She eases her head back against the headrest as she twists the volume dial. Her window is still up; for this second she does-n't care. Georgina Cherry Martin, this is your moment.

★

The wind whipped through the window, warm, sweet-scented wind. It woke her. It was ridiculously early – daybreak. She seldom saw this time of day but she loved it, the air hazy with the pending day's heat and everything to offer. Her eyes blinked, heavy from the night before. She hadn't been asleep long, maybe a few hours. Whatever it was, it wasn't good enough, not really. She stirred, contemplating rolling over and drifting off again when the breeze cut across her; this time it was heady, laced with a muskiness she knew well. A faint smile curled on her lips as the scent of his aftershave kindled an image; she could see him now without even looking, but she looked all the same; he was still there, driving, where he had been all night. Still drowsing, more asleep than awake, she surveyed him; he sat slouched against the door, his elbow resting on the frame, one hand limp around the wheel as he steered, the other lying on his lap. He was chewing; it wouldn't be gum, no doubt a bit of plastic from a pen lid or bottle top. He did that a lot. He glanced down and caught her eye; smiling an unexpected smile having found her awake for the first time in hours. She smiled slowly back, holding his gaze just long enough to tell him something that was nothing he didn't already know, before rolling over and dozing off again.

The drive was long. Endless. They had no idea where they were going or when they were going to stop.

'We'll know it when we see it,' he'd said coyly.

She'd smiled in agreement.

She awoke to the sound of gravel crunching beneath the tyres. The scent of warm tarmac gliding in through the window held a million memories, good ones. A faint twang of guilt tugged at her stomach. Not regret, there's a difference – just guilt. It might have lasted longer but his hand stroked her head and she felt nothing other than happiness. Her back was sore as she struggled up from the slouched position she had sunk into. Her muscles ached, bones crunched. She did her best to stretch her legs beneath the dashboard, her arms reaching up to the roof. It was no easy feat stretching in a car. She felt like a baby in the womb, crammed and uncomfortable. He was watching her, she could feel it. She caught him in the corner of her eye, his gaze falling between her and the road, but mostly her – alarmingly so.

'Keep them on the road mister,' she grinned, avoiding his stare and instead peering out at the view beyond her window.

She caught his smile, it warmed her.

Open fields and trees whipped by in the distance. There were no houses to be seen, just open landscape. Even the road was empty. The loneliness felt fantastic. She wanted it to stay that way, just them and the open road. No one else in existence. It was unrealistic, she knew that, but it didn't stop her from fantasising. At that second, right when it felt almost believable a lorry tore across their path, horn blaring as it flew out of a side road and into the distance ahead of them. So much for the fantasy.

Her eyes fell on him to gauge his reaction; he seemed calm, his foot seemed to have brushed the brake by instinct, but he was generally unfazed. He always was. In that second she fell in love with him a little bit more.

'I need a toilet stop, you?' he said, smiling. He could just see it; her hunkered in a field, skirt hiked up to her hips.

She hadn't bothered thinking about it until now. Darn it, there it was, the twinge. She peered around,

'There's not going to be a toilet out here, it'll be miles yet.'

His smile was coy; he had known that all along.

'Up to you,' he said. 'A man's gotta go when a man's gotta go.'

He pulled over close to a hedge and cut the engine.

'Oooh,' she moaned, her hand thrust between her thighs with the sudden urgency to wee. 'You have to keep look out, I don't want to be hooted at by some trucky.'

'Or anyone for that matter,' he smiled, looking at her in understanding. 'Don't worry, course I will. Anyway, you'll be in behind the hedge. Just pee close to it and no one will see a thing.'

'That includes you,' she said breaking into a giggle.

They wandered down a little toward a gate and hoisted themselves over, Jack first, Cherry close behind. He scouted around, the coast seemed clear. 'You go first,' he urged, turning his back to her.

She didn't argue. By now she was close to bursting. Her dress came just short of the knee; she whipped one leg out of her pants, hiked it up and crouched so low she could feel the grass graze her ass. She thanked God she wasn't in jeans; that would have been a catastrophe.

'No peeking,' she said coyly, her stare hard on his back to be sure he didn't turn and catch a glimpse of her squatting like a kid.

He wouldn't dare, it would be more than his life was worth.

'Why is it women always sound like a tap – whoosh, ' he joked as she started to pee.

'Maybe it has something to do with the lack of hose,' she jostled back, shaking herself dry and dreaming of toilet roll. She had taken it for granted much too often.

He was less reserved, turning toward the hedge, unzipping his crotch and peeing without a thought for whether she was looking or not. He didn't care. It was nothing she hadn't seen before.

She felt much better, hauling herself back over the gate and walking toward the car. He took his chance and grappled for her bum as she dashed around its nose and jumped into the passenger side, slamming the door in the process. He slid in beside her and started the engine.

'Where to, Cherry tree?' he asked with a smile. He loved how she teased. How nothing with her was easy.

'Wherever the road takes us,' she grinned, rummaging for her sunglasses and sliding them on.

They were dark glass, big-framed, her golden brown hair, wild from the wind, bouncing around their edges in loose waves.

He pushed his foot against the throttle; they were off again.

The car tore down the road, wind racing through the open windows; it exhilarated her, the air cutting across her arm as it stretched into the open road. A road that seemed endless. A road leading them too – suddenly an arch of cherry blossoms appeared in the distance; they were beautiful. He slowed, giving her time to admire them. A white butterfly caught her eye, fluttering toward a low-hanging branch. His foot was down again, the speed lighting her up from the inside out. Its wings, like tissue, crushed as it hit the windscreen. She was laughing as she saw it. She kept laughing. He always made her laugh, not because he was funny but because he made her nervous. Had she not been with him she would have felt bad for that beautiful butterfly, maybe slowed down, thought for a second. But she was and, instead, they just went faster.

There was a town in the distance; they could see it below them as they drove through the valley.

'Chipwood,' he said nodding toward it, 'first stop for an antique buyer,' he grinned.

She nodded in acknowledgement, watching as the sun caught the side of his face, the loose strands of hair ebony in the light, his swarthy skin radiant, the dark of his eyes begging her to touch him. She fought the temptation and looked away, searching blindly for the suitcase resting on the back seat. She grabbed hold of the handle and fought to drag it onto her knee. It was futile. She decided instead to unclip her belt and reach over into the back. She hadn't seen the back of the car since last night. It was laden with bags and suitcases. There was more in the boot, which carried the bigger, more desirable things. She was looking at two lives. Four actually but, she thought glancing back at him, this was the beginning.

The key for the case was tucked into her sock, hidden by the height of her boot. She tugged it free and opened it quickly enough, she hated nothing more than being in a car without her seatbelt. The zips were sticky, it had taken the two of them ten minutes to tug them closed, but she worked on them now and found they were a lot easier to open. It was something to do with the direction of the pull, not that they had done anything to improve them. It was like looking into Aladdin's cave as she flipped back the lid. Full of watches, dresser clocks, silverware, jewellery boxes, there was a pile of folded lace and another of cashmere. Some of the things they could put a rough value on but mostly they were going to be putty in some grimy dealer's hands.

'What are we going for first?' she asked.

'I don't know, nothing big, nothing obvious. Go for the silver?'

'What about trying a couple of the broaches? There's one here that's worth a good bit, I'm sure of it. The one with the stones in it?'

'If you think it's inconspicuous enough go for it but we've only been on the road a few days, we haven't got that far. Keep it safe.'

The town was bigger than they had first thought, two main streets with a square setting them apart. They parked the car on the far side so they could head straight out and with the goods in Cherry's bag, strolled back down the road in search of an antique dealers. It didn't take long.

'Antiquities and Antiques', said a small, battered sign hanging above the door.

It was small and quaint, like all the shops they'd passed. The door was old, an original they assumed by the cast-iron hinges and heavy wood. Jack led the way, his hand holding Cherry's in a tight grip as he led her into the shop. The air was thick and musty; it smelt like a million old people sitting in one room. Cherry giggled at the thought, sinking in behind Jack to compose herself. It was badly lit, gloomy except for the glow coming from various old lamps wired around the room. Some hung above their heads, others balanced precariously on tables that wobbled when touched. A fine film of dust covered the less desirable things. Others gleamed, freshly polished and eye-catching. It was like an expensive jumble sale with all manner of different items strewn together, no plan, no thought for complimenting one another.

'Hello there,' the voice broke her thought.

They turned to see a portly, middle-aged man no taller than Cherry walking toward them from the far side of the room.

'Morning sir, beautiful shop you have here,' Jack smiled, flicking his hair free from his face, revealing his gleaming teeth.

'Well I like to think so. Nice to see some youngsters appreciating it.'

Cherry took the compliment although she thought it a little far-fetched.

'You interested in anything particular?' he asked, pushing his glasses slightly down his nose.

'The opposite actually, we've come to see if you would be interested in something,' he said, Cherry stepping forward and reaching into the bag.

He appeared intrigued, open to discussion.

'Got something to show me have we?'

Jack took the silver cutlery from Cherry's grip and placed it all on the glass counter they had been led toward.

'Mr Lampton,' he said thrusting his hand toward them, Jack first then Cherry.

'Tommy,' he smiled. 'This is Sarah.'

She hadn't expected it but her thoughts moved quickly and she could see what he was doing. She was only too glad Mr Lampton had offered him his hand first or things would have gone very differently.

'A family heirloom?' he queried.

'Yes, my granny died,' Cherry said, her head hanging low, her voice quiet. She felt it again, the twang.

'These are nice, a full set of six, all matching. That's hard to find.' He looked up at them as though wondering how little he could offer. Jack caught it, they both did.

'I'll give you eighty,' he said.

'No less than one twenty'

'Okay, one?'

'One-twenty and not a penny less. There are plenty of other dealers we can take these to,' he said reaching forward to gather them up. His tone was serious; Cherry liked it, it was the tone that made her feel so protected.

'You drive a hard bargain,' Mr Lampton said, his hand yet again outstretched, this time to seal the deal.

Jack shook. They were £120 better off.

'Anything else in there to show me?' he asked, a spark of greed in his eye.

'I'm not sure it's really your thing,' Jack teased, glancing around, his weight already on his heel, ready to leave.

'Try me.'

Cherry reached into the bag and drew out a broach. It was simple, silver frame, portrait setting; it was old, very old. She knew from what she had heard that a broach of this variety could fetch them a few hundred from the right buyer.

He inspected it closely, taking his time with the silver marking before making an offer well below what they expected.

'No thank you, we'll hold on to this one. I think we can both say we are happy,' said Jack, slipping the broach back into the bag and leading Cherry toward the door. 'Good doing business with you.'

'Good day to you both,' Mr Lampton called after them, already engrossed in his new cutlery set.

Jack slipped his hand around Cherry's waist and drew her close as they hit the curb. 'This is our first stop, if we can't do better than that further down the road. We'll settle but we're not going to take that first time. You agree?'

She looked up at him and smiled. 'Absolutely. We're doing well enough.' The bulge in his trousers caught her eye. She slipped her fingers in and pulled out a note. 'Breakfast?'

'Next stop,' he said, the dimple in his right cheek sinking back to expose itself.

'Next stop,' she echoed, remembering the before.

This was the now. The before was everything leading up to it.

They smiled; it was wicked.